The Three Kings of Ybor

Volume 2: The Wolves of the Syndicate

Written By Rock Kitaro

www.StageInTheSky.com

Copyright 2014

Cover photo provided by Jen Poblete
& Brandy Scaglione of Exposition Photography

Recap of "The Three Kings of Ybor – Volume 1: Eliza Christie's Vendetta"

Fifteen-year-old Eliza Christie ventures to the slums of Ybor City looking for information on Braden Pierce, the assassin who she believes killed her father. As expected, she finds trouble in the form of a biker gang who weren't above the temptation of indulging in rape. Unexpectedly, she finds a hero in a mysterious drifter named Gavin Hassell. Convinced that Eliza would never give up her pursuit for Braden, Gavin injects her with the Furyx Gene. This gene modification performance enhancer grants her enhanced strength, speed, durability and heightened senses.

With enough on his plate as it is, Angel Gazi, one of the city's few honest detectives and Eliza's legal guardian sends the rebellious teen to live with his sister in Korea. Boa Gazi takes in Eliza with the hopes of providing a loving stable family environment to shake her of her vindictive nature. And it works…for a while.

That is until Eliza witnesses Boa's nomadic husband practicing ninjitsu in the backyard. Thus, a Pandora's Box has been opened with Eliza now suddenly obsessed with learning martial arts.

Then, on her sixteenth birthday the flooding emotions of her late father and insatiable need for vengeance comes rushing back. She skips school and wanders into Seoul hoping to clear her head, searching for some sort of internal solution. Her serenity is broken when she sees a group of blade-wielding cooks chasing a student. She impulsively intervenes and easily thrashes them like ragdolls. Only, Eliza doesn't leave once the deed is done. She doesn't run away or try to explain herself. With defiance and a sizzling sense of satisfaction, Eliza just sits there waiting for the police to come and take her away.

Table of Contents

Warning: The following volume contains graphic violence and plausible profanity.

Chapter 6 – "August the 18th"

Eliza spent six hours in jail before Boa arrived to pick her up at a little past eight. The police were still baffled as to how she managed to put eight grown men in the intensive care unit. Four men required emergency surgery to drain internal bleeding and all eight needed chiropractors to set bones back in place. Not to mention the months of physical therapy and rehab every one of them would eventually need.

The witnesses gave statements to the news reporters on site and her photo was broadcasted on the evening news. It was hard to believe that she took them on unarmed and many suspected that she was carrying concealed metal plates under her socks and sleeves. Despite the negative context of the reporters trying to drum up sympathy towards the workers, Eliza was the hero of the day.

It turned out that the college student she saved was the son of a wealthy city councilman, thus the unbelievable charges of aggravated assault and battery were dropped. She also didn't have to worry about the forty-five million won worth of medical expenses. The seafood workers chalked that bill up to worker's comp.

Before Boa arrived, Eliza pretty much expected a display of disappointment and anger. Instead, it was one of deep sadness and pity. Boa was dressed warm in a pair of blue jeans, a beige sweater and an oversized purple bubble coat as if she had just thrown the attire together last minute.

As they stood together in the lobby, Boa signed a release to check Eliza out at the front desk while the receptionist returned Eliza's belongings. She was allowed to keep her green hooded overcoat with her in the cell, but her mp3 player, wallet, pocketknife and bracelet would remain confiscated for a period of two weeks. The receptionist examined Eliza's ID before giving it back to her.

"Oh. Happy Birthday." The receptionist said nonchalantly. Eliza rolled her eyes as she snatched back her wallet.

A gasp chimed out with Boa arching her eyebrows in genuine shock. "Eliza... It's your birthday?"

Eliza scoffed. "Yes, Boa. What of it?"

Boa pouted and held her hands over her heart. "Eliza! Why? Why didn't you say anything?"

"Oh my god! It's not a big deal. Jesus, can we go!?" Eliza shouted as she stormed toward the front exit.

Boa bowed with respect to the receptionist before following Eliza out the front doors. The receptionist stood shaking her head. The comical scowl of contempt couldn't be helped. In the back of her mind, she was wishing Eliza was her daughter so she could discipline her properly.

There was a cold front moving through with temperatures already dropping to a nerve-wrecking twenty-eight degrees. On the second-floor parking garage, Eliza was leaning against the dark purple SUV with her arms crossed. Waiting…brooding…

As she trudged up the stairs to the second level and past the two rows of vehicles… Boa was almost as confused as she was in a state of disparity. For months now, she's been under the impression that Eliza was adjusting well to a new Korean life. That she was happy with the children and getting along well in school. But it seemed that her inner demons were alive and running free. She had only chained them away for so long…but once again, they've escaped.

"Let's go!" Eliza shouted, holding back the urge to call her an unpleasant female dog.

With a deep sigh of hopelessness, Boa unlocked the doors with her remote control and turned the ignition. Eliza hopped in and slammed her door shut. The force of the door closing caused Boa to stop in her tracks. Boa thought that she might have heard glass cracking from Eliza's door and a subtle trace of terror washed over her. It was only then that she realized how much she had no idea what kind of person Eliza was. The apprehensive thoughts of what Eliza might be capable of was enough to make anyone cautious. She had to tread softly. From opening the door and buckling her seatbelt, Boa's every move was delicate and free of any attitude that could provoke offense.

She drove with caution through the busy downtown district of Gangnam. The congested traffic both vehicular and pedestrian provided ample time for Boa to gather the strength needed to be a firm parent. But the mystery surrounding what she could possibly by thinking was unnerving. It's been straight silence with the radio off for ten minutes.

…

"How long do you plan to keep this up?" Boa said soft and timidly.

With her arms folded, Eliza slowly turned with her signature squinting glare. "Excuse me?"

"I'm just wondering. How long do you plan on hating the world for what has happened to you?" Boa told her.

Eliza scoffed with a malicious smile. "Please… You've got to be one of the most obliviously stupid guppies I've ever met. And believe me I've run into a lot of em. Where's your husband at? Hmm? Where has he been all these months? Do you know? Do you even care? Or is it you're so hopeful and stupidly optimistic that it's made you blind to the double life he leads. Probably working for some kkangpae and screwing every other slut he sees walking about. You don't know me, alright? Just worry about yours before coming at me with that afterschool special load of horseshit."

Each vitriolic syllable was scathing. Her bold authoritative declaration completely overwhelmed Boa to the point that she was speechless. It was astounding how deep the words dug through. Boa knew she was a very trusting of others, but she didn't think of herself as oblivious or stupid. And from the continuous slur words that came out like a fire hose, Boa could discern that Eliza had so much to say for so long. The pity she felt for the sulking teenager was understandable. The habit of thinking the worse about everyone… it must have been so lonely for her all those months in Korea. And she kept it all bottled up to herself.

Still hot and bothered, Eliza was breathing hard with her gaze brooding ahead. She began to notice that they weren't driving towards the house on the hills but on the opposite side of the city.

"Where are we going?" Eliza asked.

"Do you know what a romanticist is?" Boa asked calmly.

Eliza rubbed her cold palms together as she let out a loud frustrated sigh. "For crying out loud, just answer the damn question." She uttered.

"There." Boa said, nodding her head in Eliza's direction.

Eliza looked to her right. She was so disturbed and irritated with Boa that she didn't realize they were next to Han River on the rim of Seocho. Over the river, the Banpo Bridge stretched to grant commuters passage from the districts of Seocho to Yongsan. The Banpo Bridge was a national landmark that has stood fully functional for over 200 years. The feature that made it special was that it was fully lit, spouting the Moonlight Rainbow Fountain. The fountain was an arrangement of ten thousand multicolored LED nozzles that spanned the entire length just under the ledge on both sides. The nozzles were attached to rows of water pumps that spouted over 200 tons of recycled water a minute. The bright colored streaks of water shot out as far as fifty meters horizontally from both sides of the bridge.

It was a breathtaking sight. Even Eliza with all of her pent up hate and animosity couldn't help but feel a wave of stress discharge from her body. It was a perfect backdrop in variations of velvet and purple with the rainbow-colored sprays of water shooting towards it. The Banpo Bridge was built over the top of the older pre-existing Jamsu Bridge so it looked double-decker. Once fully functional for vehicles to alleviate traffic, the Jamsu was now a brightly lit walkway for pedestrians to fully take in the view of Banpo from underneath. Boa felt a nice walk with beautiful scenery might do the both of them so good.

Boa drove the SUV in to a river walk parking lot and turned off the engine. Eliza said nothing as she exited the vehicle and headed towards the walkway. Boa just sat there, still contemplating what to do. She could see Eliza through the windshield, tightening the opening of her green overcoat hoodie as she stared out toward the water. On some subconscious level, Boa admired Eliza's independent nature. Eliza was by herself with no one around her. With no one else in her life who she believed cared for her. And yet, she didn't seem at all bothered by that fact.

Such a spirit…

Just then, an idea surfaced. Determined to get through to her no matter what, Boa reached over for the glove compartment and opened it. Amongst her registration and insurance information, was a small photo album of her children and a thick green book. Boa grabbed the green book and closed the glove compartment. Briefly flipping through the pages, a happy smirk of nostalgia washed over Boa. Eliza was squinting at her from the outside. Boa smiled at her and let out a soft high-pitch chuckle of glee as she hugged the book.

"I'll conquer you yet, Miss Elizabeth!" Boa thought aloud with a haughty lift of her chin.

She exited the vehicle and zipped up her purple bubble coat. Then, she walked past Eliza with that same haughty smile as if she didn't care what Eliza thought of her. It was so funny. Eliza was so much more taller than Boa, and from the way the two were dressed, it was understandable to confuse which of them was the guardian. Boa finally looked back and gestured for Eliza to join her. And with that, the two walk down the paved cement steps toward the covered Jamsu Bridge, sticking close to the railing for an unobstructed view of the glass calm river.

Eliza noticed the book Boa was carrying and lamented the thought of her doing any more lecturing, but Boa began anyway. "I can't stand here and pretend to know how you feel, Ms. Christie."

"Then please. Don't." Eliza uttered. Her obvious disdain had no effect on Boa. She just kept smiling with her arms wrapped around the thick green book.

"When I married Hideo twelve years ago, my family completely cut me off. This was even before we moved here. When we were still living in Apollo Beach. They never officially disowned me, but you could tell they were cutting me off. Just through e-mails they'd forward to one another about one of my cousin's marriages or any newborn babies. Or how happy their visits were to one another, I was ostracized." Boa said.

"Because he was a fugitive?" Eliza asked.

Boa shook her head no. "Hideo is a fugitive because he dodged Japan's mandatory military service requirement of all males. Such a meaningless offense that strips away an individual's free will. Hideo is a rebel by nature. He isn't the type of man to lay down his life for anything or anyone he doesn't believe in. The idea of old men talking with young men dying didn't sit well with him and his cousins. So they left the country. I supported Hideo's decision whole-heartedly."

"No, I'm mixed descendant of Puerto Ricans and Cubans. There's a lot in my blood but predominantly Latino, Central American blood. You'd think because whites are no longer a majority with races being so blended, it wouldn't matter what color he was. But because he was Japanese, my papa said no." Boa explained.

Boa snickered. "Since Cloud was born, I've yet to receive a single phone call or letter. Not from my hundreds of cousins, dozens of aunt or uncles, grandparents, or even my own parents."

As Boa explained, a sulking frown transitioned over and you could see the furls of her nostrils. Eliza briefly held her breath as she stared at the housewife. In the near five months she's been living with Boa, she's never seen anything come remotely close to the serious display of ire and animosity that was written across Boa's pure and innocent face. Not even when Cloud broke his window trying to escape in the middle of the night, or when Rain painted multiplication tables on the oven hatch. The most Boa ever displayed was a heavy sigh with raised eyebrows of despair. Never anger.

"I hated them. I hated everyone. To be abandoned and neglected. Just me, Hide, and my children all alone on this huge unstable planet…I can't say I know how it feels to have my father taken from me. But I know how it feels to have both your mother and father turn their backs on you as if you were already dead to them." Said Boa.

Eliza sympathized. It would've been self-centered and downright rude for Eliza to compare her tragedy to Boa's even though she knew she wanted to. The revelation didn't make Eliza feel any better. Instead, it only frustrated her further. As if she now had no right to criticize Boa, even though she knew she wanted to.

"Not even Gazi?" Eliza asked.

"Angel was a different man back then. Ask yourself, did you even know he had a sister before he told you that you were coming to live here?" Boa said with a depressing strain in her breath.

Eliza crossed her arms and rubbed her shoulders as a cold gust ran through. And she felt compelled to ask, "So then, how did you deal with it all? I've never once seen you raise your voice or catch a fit. Do you? Like…do you storm off into the woods and wail on some tree branches or somethin?"

Boa giggled as she finally held up the book she was carrying. It was a medium-size hardcover book that was half as thick as the Itaewon phone directory. Initially, Eliza was disheartened to see that Boa had found inspiration in a book. Eliza had heard stories of people reading religious books to pull themselves out from their personal hells. Subconsciously, Eliza thought it was weak of anyone to not just deal with their problems on their own. She doubted the existence of any book that could possibly remove the large stain on her heart.

The two ladies were already an eighth of the way down Jamsu Bridge. The long range sprays of water cascading overhead brought in a light freezing mist that landed softly on their faces. There weren't so many pedestrians, only less than thirty that were spread out amongst the length of the bridge. There was one gathering of five young adults, holding their own break-dancing session. There were even some teens, younger than Eliza, trying to pull off flip tricks with their skateboards. But it was more so a romantic spot where it wasn't unusual to see couples holding hands along the railing. Nevertheless, Eliza and Boa had managed to find a secluded spot where no one could overhear their conversation.

"When I was little, there was a kind, warm-hearted social activist named Reginald Harvey. He used to give motivational speeches at my middle school and high school. He wasn't self-righteous so to speak, but he was just a man with strong morals, believing in the philosophies of historical peace men like Martin Luther King Jr. and Gandhi. Have you heard of them?" Boa asked.

"Um…vaguely. Harvey sounds familiar. Did he live in Tampa?" Eliza asked.

"Yes, actually. I had the fortunate opportunity to confide in him a lot." Boa said.

"You confided in some motivational speaker? Isn't that a little weird? Not to mention creepy? Was he into you or something?" Eliza asked.

"No, no, no, Eliza. I know when you think of Tampa Bay, you'd normally have to ask yourself those kinds of questions just to get by, but Mr. Harvey was different. When you're a child, there are not many adults who take you seriously. To me, it was extremely valuable to have someone who didn't look down on me because of my age, but saw me as his equal despite his popularity and superior maturity, patience, and wisdom." Boa explained.

Boa handed the book over to Eliza. Eliza wore a look that said, "no thanks," but reluctantly accepted it.

"Before Mr. Harvey died, he wrote that book. It's called August the 18th. Angel knew we were close so he sent me a copy."

Eliza opened the book and noticed a signature signed in ink on the front flap. The signature was personalized to Boa. It answered the question as to why she didn't have a digital copy. The pages and Times New Roman font used in its black typing…it was nostalgic. Eliza gradually began to grasp the connection Boa had, not just to the book, but also with the man who wrote it.

"What's it about, Boa?"

The freezing weather getting the best of her, Boa reached into her purse and took out a pair of purple wool mittens to put on. Then she began.

"It's about a leader who grows up never being able to celebrate his own birthday. Because his parent's religion was against it. They used religious guilt to oppress him for years, keeping him from doing things like socializing with peers who were outside of that religion. Keeping him from watching and listening to the same media his classmates listened to. Everyone else around him grew up with a normal childhood so the envy made him a lonely, angry child. He didn't have any friends to talk to because they misread the boy to be arrogant and too good to do what they were doing. He couldn't talk to his parents because they were the source of his agitation. It finally came to a point where he didn't care if God hated him or not. He started to become what others accused him to be because what's the point in fighting it? In his teens he rebelled, hating not only religion but society in general. He picked fights and disrespected all forms of authority, secretly hoping someone had the strength to take him on and end his life."

"After spending years abroad and learning about centuries of history and cultures that have previously been hidden and buried by years of destruction and warfare, the man decides to create his own tradition, a movement called Indivisualism. The visual in it is spelled like visual arts. Like your own vision." Boa explained.

"You see Eliza, this future romanticist leader learned to accept himself by acknowledging that it's okay to feel certain emotions even though society deem them to be inappropriate, unholy, or plain wrong. It's acting on those emotions that initiates damage and distributes chaos onto the world. That's why feelings like revenge and jealousy are cast in such a dim light. But those feelings are there for a reason. Revenge and jealousy gives birth to motivation. Without such motivation, change could never take place for better or worse." Boa told her.

Boa stood behind Eliza and put both arms around her. The added warmth from her body was very welcomed as Eliza's tense shoulders gradually began to descend. Sprays of green and red water shot out like fire hoses from the bridge above them. And suddenly…tenderly…Boa instructed the blonde sixteen-year-old to close her eyes.

Eliza grinned, amused by the theatrics. "Why, Boa?"

"Just do it. The effect will be more memorable if you do as I say." Boa chuckled.

Eliza scoffed as if she wasn't interested, when in fact, she enjoyed that pleasant feeling of anticipating surprise. As instructed, she closed her eyes and awaited what Boa had in store. The gushing sounds of running water filled her head and the freezing mist upon her tan cheeks and nose suddenly didn't feel so frozen anymore.

Boa moved closer to Eliza's ears and whispered.

"…imagine..."

"Imagine that you're in a lush beautiful green clearing in the woods. It's a bright, sunny day with plenty of large fluffy clouds. There's a melodic tune from a piano playing in the distance but there isn't a piano in sight. The scent of white gardenias takes over you as we frolic through the meadows with a strong refreshing breeze caressing our dresses. It's not hot. It's not cold. It's perfect. You can feel the moisture of the dew beneath your feet as we skip over the healthy green grass. Do you have it?"

Eliza nodded with a bright smile, flashing her pearly whites.

"The right path is the path I choose. I see people as individuals, separated from age, race, gender, orientation, stereotype, ethnicity or religion."

"Got it?" Boa asked. Eliza nodded.

"Well done! Now imagine that the sun has fallen and its now night time. You and I are sitting on a soft dry grassy hill-top overlooking the wavy sea." Boa said.

Eliza couldn't help but laugh out loud. Boa giggled with her as she reminded her to keep her eyes closed. Eliza clinched her eyelids tighter as she insisted that they were.

"We're on that grassy hill. We can hear the majestic roars of the waves crashing against the rocky cliffs beneath us. We look up from the vast horizon of nothing but ocean. The clear night sky is filled with millions of stars as visible and bright like glittery white dust on a violet sky. Do you see it?" Boa whispered in her soft voice.

"I see it." Eliza giggled.

Boa chanted. "Indivisualism is not an organization but a movement. It's a sense of feeling, a self-acknowledgment of freedom from traditions and customs. An indivisualist blames no other human, entity, or circumstance for their mistakes. They are in control of their own world and accept responsibility for their actions."

"Now open your eyes."

Eliza opened her eyes as she was instructed. They were heavy with tears and nothing could prevent a trail from rolling down her cold soft cheeks. The cascading flow of water…for some reason they seemed more beautiful than before. She let out a heavy sigh as she turned around in Boa's arms and looked into her soft brown eyes.

"Eliza, it's a state of complete honesty. An indivisualist is true to herself above all else. True to her emotions. True to her heart. True to her conscience."

Boa stepped to the side of Eliza and approached to lean over the railing of the river. Eliza looked down at the book and rubbed her thumb over the leather texture of the front cover.

"True to her conscience?" Eliza asked, almost in a soft involuntary nature.

"The best way to deal with internal conflicts is obvious. They say that sometimes the best hiding places are right in front of you. Out in the open. But most people are too blind to see what's in front of them. Or rather, too afraid to admit it." Boa told her.

Eliza's eyes watered with an intense gaze as she flailed her arms out of desperate frustration. "Damn it Boa! Admit what?"

Boa stretched her arms vertically to the sky, taking a full view of the Banpo's undercarriage. With a deep sigh, she put an arm around Eliza and kissed her forehead. "To admit what you selfishly want. Once you're completely honest with yourself, I have no doubts that you'll turn that fury to something more productive."

And just like that, Eliza's heart skipped a beat. The words had penetrated her cognitive and rattled her to the core. It was as if time had stood still with only a single spotlight focused on her. She couldn't believe it. All this time she was aware of the fact that she was brave and courageous in the face of others…but to herself… Was she hiding?

Boa and Eliza turned around to walk back to the SUV. The newly turned sixteen-year-old was silent the whole trip back. Even before they reached home, Eliza was already ten pages into "August the 18th". At dinner, Cloud and Rain were both curious and found it amusing to see Eliza reading a printed book at the table. Boa allowed it, fully satisfied and convinced that she had finally gotten through to her. To top it all off, she even served warm pecan pie for Eliza's birthday.

At half past one in the morning, Eliza woke up more eager than all of her days in Korea. It was a Saturday morning, so she didn't have to worry about Rain or Boa disturbing her for the next ten to twelve hours. Wearing her light-green jogging suit under her green overcoat, Eliza sat Indian-style on the back patio under a porch light, still reading Mr. Harvey's works. The spell it cast over her was allowed her to ignore the below freezing weather. That and the fact that there was no wind. The trees on the mountain were all still and calm as if they were part of a painting under the moonlight.

"Human life, above all things, is the most precious thing on earth."

After pondering the words, Eliza scoffed to herself and said out loud. "Yeah, I beg to differ."

Deep within the forest at about a 120 fifty yards out, someone was watching Eliza. It was Hideo, fully clothed in his black ninja attire, standing on a steep perch along the hillside. After studying her closely for well over ten minutes, Hide simply closed his eyes and shook his head. Just as he turned around to walk away, Hide stepped on a small dry twig that let out a slight crackle. Eliza's ears twitched as if she just heard a gunshot from the forest. Her eyes shot wide open before an enthusiastic grin of ambition flashed over.

"Hmph! Got you!"

Dropping her book, Eliza whipped off her overcoat and sweat jacket to sprint off towards the forest of Bukhansan wearing only her shoes, her sweatpants and a revealing black sports bra. After shouldering through a thick brush of bushes with the strong aroma of pine in the air, Eliza spotted her target on a hiking pathway over 300 meters away.

With only the luminescence of moonlight, Eliza used her Furyx-induced speed to sprint down the forest pathway. Within fifteen seconds, Eliza covered the 300 meters to find a steep hill at the end of the path where she knew Hide jumped down. Then, there was no sign of Hide anywhere. Trusting her instincts, Eliza jumped off the edge of the path to slide down the sloping grass covered hills before regaining control and taking off in a run again.

At the bottom of the hill was a wide but shallow stream that served as a mirror for the moon. Several smooth boulders the size of basketballs breached the surface of the stream. Without breaking stride, Eliza ran down the hill and leaped over fifteen feet to cover the distance to land like a cat on the boulders. She hopped from one to another till she was on the banks of the other side.

Quickly scanning the area, her vision picked up footprints in the mud heading toward a sloping face of another vegetated hillside covered with countless winding cedar trees. Eliza dashed off in that direction.

Ducking under tree branches and leaping over their limbs, Eliza picked up the pace across the hillside. While in midstride, she caught sight of not just Hide, but four other ninjas that ran alongside him. They were using hooks and grappling wires to swing from branch to branch high above her. Eliza's light complexion running at super speed in the moonlight caught Hide's attention. He knew she was following him, but thought he lost her back at the stream. He hand-signaled to the four ninjas to disperse away from him onto different paths.

Eliza slid to grinding halt in the freezing wet soil as she saw the ninjas swinging off the given path. Instinctively, she managed to keep her eyes on Hide and followed him. Their sense of awareness of their surroundings impressed Eliza and she wondered if they were using some kind enhancers. Without even realizing it, a smile of pure glee and excitement curled from ear to ear.

With her attention focused upward toward the trees, she didn't pick up on the small glimmer of light that just flashed from below. There was a horizontal tripwire set up three inches off the ground across the path just ahead of her. Eliza's shins hit the thin wire and the trap was sprung. A large spiked log came swinging towards her from the right. After letting out a sharp gasp, Eliza quickly dove and rolled forward, narrowly missing the log that swung by.

"Oh! You have got to be shitting me!" Eliza let out.

Her uncovered shoulders and back were covered in layer of sweat and wet soil. Understandably, frustration was beginning to set in. After unleashing a pounding punch onto the soil, she took off in full sprint hoping to catch sight of them again.

Failing to learn from her mistake, Eliza's vision was so focused on zooming into hundreds of meters away that she missed yet another wire. After tripping the wire, a 10x10 foot brick trap door that was made to camouflage in with the surrounding ground quickly slid off to the side to reveal a massive twenty foot drop. With Eliza's speed, she was able to jump at the last second to reach and grab the edge other side.

"What the hell?!" Eliza blurted out, slightly wondering what would happen if a child had tripped the wire.

After pulling herself up, she finally took the time to continue with caution. Staying silent, her eyes were peeled for anything. She couldn't see them anywhere so she stepped lightly, focusing her hearing on any sudden sounds. After a brief moment of hearing nothing but the various medleys of insects, Eliza stopped where she was and stood in place, looking around at the different trees and catching a glimpse of the filtered full moon through their barren winter branches.

There was dirt in her blond her blonde hair, she was breathing hard and her face was moist with sweat. Then…with an inexplicable smile, she uttered something to herself.

"Oh crap."

She had just come to the realization that she was completely lost. Putting her hands on her hips, Eliza walked aimless in one direction, believing that if she just followed it, concentrating on staying in that direction so she wouldn't fall into the archaic comical sketch of walking in circles.

Eliza walked for a full hour and twenty minutes before hopelessness began to set in. But with Eliza, her reaction to such hopelessness wasn't like the miserable dread most people would experience. Eliza just kept smirking, sporadically letting out a loud chuckle. She thought it was truly funny how quickly she dropped that book and ran off. She imagined how silly it would've been to any bystander who saw her do that.

Finally, she came to a large clearing in the forest. It was a flat plain displaying a field of knee-high grass that came up to her knees and surrounded by the oak trees and unkempt bushes. She exhaled deeply as she was about to wipe her sweaty forehead but stopped because her palms were dirty. She reached for her shirt before realizing that she wasn't wearing a shirt. The sweat and mud on her breast and stomach was beginning to freeze. And just as she was bending over to rest her hand on her knees, two bright torches were lit behind her.

Startled, Eliza instinctively leaped forward and spun 180 degrees in midair, covering twelve feet the single stride. There were two ninjas holding the torches while three others stood between them. There was also another smaller figure dressed in a ninja outfit and it didn't take Eliza long to deduce that it had to be Cloud. After just witnessing Eliza pull off that incredible leap, the ninjas were exchanging glances of skepticism.

One by one, the ninjas removed their facemasks. As expected, Eliza recognized Hide in the middle of the five with Cloud by his side. She was stunned, however, to see that the other men all had the sunbaked loose-skinned faces of those who had to be in their mid to late forties. Much older than the energetic agile young ninjas she thought she was chasing. The four men were Hide's Japanese relatives. All bearing the same conservative short buzz cuts.

After a brief standoff of awkward silence with everyone staring at one another, Eliza finally broke ice as she softly whispered, "Mr. Hideo…"

The oldest looking ninja with strains of grey peppered hair rolled his eyes. "Who does this one think she is?" **Eutaka** grunted in Japanese.

"My wife's brother's orphan. I apologize on her behalf. Seems my premonition was correct after all." Hideo answered while keeping his eyes on Eliza.

"Still. It's a wonder she's gotten this far." **Kamiyama** said with a tone that suggested he was impressed.

"The Furyx Gene. I told you guys about it. It's the only explanation. She's American for Christ's sake." **Maeda** barked.

"The Furyx Gene? Are you serious? Where would someone like her get a hold of that stuff? Didn't you say people were being killed and kidnapped for it?" Kamiyama asked Maeda.

"It is the only explanation, Kamiyama-san." Hide responded, still staring at Eliza.

"So, what do we do?" **Takumi,** the youngest of them asked.

That whole time, the ninjas were communicating in Japanese. While Eliza couldn't understand a word, she knew body language and identified the abrasiveness in their tones. There was only so much her patience could take.

"Hide-san... Ask her what she wants." Eutaka instructed.

Annoyed, Hide let out deep sigh before he uttered in English, "Eliza? What do you want?"

Eliza scoffed, insulted by his bluntness. She approached them with a salty attitude as if she was going to return an order that the server got wrong.

"I've been waiting to see you for months, Mr. Hide! You're never home, you douche! GOD!" Eliza shouted as loud as she could before pausing to get a hold of herself.

"Look, I remember what you said about finding the best and imitating them. Well, I've seen what this city has to offer, and I want to learn ninjitsu."

Cloud was the only one to find Eliza amusing. Her demands were followed by a comical round of scoffs and sucked teeth from the ninjas. Everyone was eye checking her from the absurdity of her request.

"Ninjitsu isn't for kids." Eutaka chimed out in perfect English.

Eliza gasped with bewilderment while shooting all of the fingers on her right hand to point at Cloud.

"Cloud Shikagane is a prodigy. Ninjitsu has flowed in his veins for centuries. Unlike the Furyx that runs through yours. Don't Lie!" Maeda told her, also speaking perfect English.

Hide calmly lowered Maeda's arm that was pointing at the teenager. And Eliza's own bewildered expression became more contorted with the question as to how they could've possibly heard of Furyx all the way out here.

"Don't deny it, wench. If you weren't hyped up on that crutch, we would've lost you a long way back." Maeda barked.

"Wench? Wait a second! How on earth do you guys know about that?" Eliza asked with a squint of her green eyes.

"We're fugitives, kid. We know everything there is to know below the surface." Takumi said with a blatant saturation of pride that his relatives always found unbecoming.

"Yeah, well I'm here now." Eliza snapped. "I recognize that you guys are the best, so teach me!"

The ninjas snickered amongst themselves. "No fucking way." Maeda told her.

"Yeah. Turn around and run back home, Madonna." Takumi joined before laughing out loud with Maeda.

Kamiyama watched as Eliza's ambitious shoulders gradually sink under his cousins' words. "Come on guys. She could've been seriously injured. If our contraptions couldn't stop her, what makes you think your words will?" Kamiyama said before shooting an inspirational wink Eliza's way.

"Kamiyama's ex-wife was a white woman." Takumi said in Japanese.

The men laughed as Kamiyama glared at Takumi, his forehead tilted forward, his thick bushy eyebrows raised. "Takumi! You watch your tongue!"

Throughout the duration of their exchanges, Hide didn't laugh, nor did he shift his unwavering gaze from the girl. Knowing her attitude would have no effect on the man with the natural born poker face, Eliza simply submitted to wait for his definite answer. The desperation in her green eyes was both unnerving and frightening. He didn't have an extensive amount of experience with teenagers…but to Hide, there was something about her that didn't even seem human. It was as if he was staring into the eyes of a chained jaguar that was begging to be set free.

After a brief round of laughter from his brethren, Hide finally raised his hand to silence them. He then stepped forward and stood merely an inch taller than her. From Eliza's view, the moon was directly behind him, so all she saw was the silhouette of his figure with two torches on both sides of him.

"Elizabeth. Why do this?" Hide began. "Before you answer, I want you to think. I don't want to hear that you want to learn self-defense or appreciate the arts. It's very offensive and stupid to hear lies like that. The truth, young one. In the grand scheme of things, why would you want to put yourself through the rigorous training and years of self-torture to learn this discipline? Why do you desire to be the best? Speak!"

Eliza saline glossed eyes moved in an erratic fashion as she searched for the right words to say. She wondered how Hide would react to the truth. Or if she even knew what the truth was. She deliberated about coming up with a lie, but with Hide…Deception seemed futile.

In a sudden change of character, Eliza put the men on edge as she slowly closed her eyes and exhaled deeply through her nostrils. Finally…not only was she beginning to take the men seriously…but herself as well. In a brief state of meditation she allowed herself to escape and transport back to that grassy hill under the stars with Boa. Eliza smiled as she remembered Boa's spoken words. Her soft humble voice chimed deep within Eliza's cognitive.

"The best way to deal with internal conflicts is obvious. But most people are too afraid to admit it. To admit what they selfishly want."

Still smiling, Eliza opened her eyes. Everyone wore a puzzled yet amused expression that Eliza would've found hilarious on any other occasion. But instead of laughing at them, she took in another deep breath and locked her eyes with Hideo's.

"Mr. Hide. The answer is obvious. I want justice for my father's murder. You can call it revenge. You can call it childish. You can say that the justice I speak of isn't even justice at all. But the cold cut truth is that I just don't give a damn. I'd rather be satisfied in hell than miserable in heaven." Eliza declared boldly without skipping a beat or stuttering in tone.

The men were taken aback. Only Hide's poker face stayed the same, not swayed even in the slightest. He casually averted his eyes to look down at his son. With a slight grin, he nodded at the boy and rubbed the top of his head. The bond between the father and son was strong. He didn't need to speak to translate his intentions and Cloud giggled, clearly and accurately interpreting his intentions. He untied a package that was strapped around his shoulder in a dark cloth and handed it to his father.

An inexplicable tingling feeling of excitement overcame Eliza as she watched Hide unwrap the dark cloth. The package was a short katana sword. The sheath was made of white ivory and decorated in an elegant design of light-green poison ivy leaves. Hide unsheathed the sword in a swift smooth motion to reveal the glistening blade of folded steel. From its black handle to the tip of the blade, its total length measured out to eighteen inches. Hide held it up horizontally, pivoting his wrist to feel for its center of balance. Satisfied with the weapon's craftsmanship, Hide slid the blade back into its sheath.

"My wife tells me you like light-green. This sword is called, Ivy." Hide said.

Eliza was ecstatic but put up a front to hide her happiness. So she let out a faint, "yes" that was barely audible. With both hands, she reached out and gratefully accepted the weapon. The men all grinned in their own personal signs of approval. Takumi and Maeda were especially pleased with their performances. They knew all along that they'd be accepting Eliza. It was just their twisted sense of humor to put her through the ringer.

"As your sensei!" Hide barked sternly, snapping Eliza out of a covetous trance. "I only have one demand in taking you in. Do you understand?"

Eliza nodded humbly.

"One's resolve is a strong element to their character. What makes a character even stronger, is their ability to adjust their resolve in light of new circumstances. It is deplorable to remain intransigent and it hinders one's personal growth. I'm not asking you to promise you'll change. But you must promise to remember these words. Never become stagnant. Constantly move. This is the Shikagane way. Promise me!" Hide told her.

Eliza's eyes swelled, overwhelmed with immense pride as she dropped to her knees in the cold soil. With her hands clinching the ivory scabbard of the sword, she looked up to the men and swore that she'd never forget it. Hide sighed at the sheer amount of work that he knew was cut out for him.

And yet…There was no doubt in his mind that Eliza wouldn't give up or quit in her training. Like Gavin before him, there was an eager subconscious sense of guilty pleasure in wondering what Eliza would do with her ability. And as expected, Eliza would never waiver in her ambition to be the best. Within four years she was able to master the Shikagane style of ninjitsu when it would normally take decades for most men. Living with Boa, Cloud, and Rain, Eliza was able to finally able to taste what it was like to live with a traditional family.

"August the 18th" became Eliza's personal bible. She ended up memorizing the book after reading it cover to cover twenty-eight times. Each time she read it, she found a new interpretation, a hidden message, a new principle, and more importantly, something she could relate to. By the time Eliza Christie was eighteen, she had graduated high school in the top of her class. Being able to memorize formulas and dates with just one look had its advantage.

Following her graduation, Eliza took a year off from her studied to devote her training to Hideo's martial arts full time. She helped out Boa around the house by walking Rain and Cloud to and from school. And Boa even began paying Eliza as her capoeira assistant. In May of 2206, Eliza received an acceptance letter from the world-renowned Tampa Metropolitan University. After being away for four years, she figured it was about time for her to make a comeback. Thus, the first six chapters were only a prelude to the hurricane of disruption Eliza was about to unleash.

One of the last things Eliza said to Boa before she walked through the terminal for her flight back to the American Empire was a quote from Reginald Harvey's "August the 18th."

"The reason why things are just the way they are is because everyone talks about change without putting forth action. I will never settle for this life, with the idea that these are the cards I've been dealt. The only thing that is certain is that at some point we all die. But until then, this is my life. It belongs to me and nobody else."

Chapter 7 – The Pierce Syndicate

…August, 2206…

With a population of 34 million, Tampa Bay was the largest agglomeration in the world and it was still expanding. Once nicknamed, the Cigar City over two hundred years ago, it now carried the stigma of being referred to by intransigent historians as the "New New York" or simply "The Kingdom." City officials even changed the name of the actual bay to "Bay of Tampa" just so the Greater Area and all of its surrounding townships and districts could be known the whole world over as simply Tampa Bay instead of an isolated Tampa, Clearwater, St. Petersburg, etcetera. Needless to say, it was an extravagant cultural center that was booming in diversity, architectural achievements and renaissance.

With the global climate change that froze most of the northern hemisphere, the worst kinds of natural disasters the current inhabitants had to contend with were spectacular lightning storms and the occasional blizzards that often flooded the rivers and districts below sea level. Thankfully, the archaic days of hurricane induced disasters were next to non-existent. Thus the empire's most developed metropolis was able to blossom into a network of elaborate bridges that stretched over the dozens waterways. And in the heart of the scenic downtown Tampa cityscape were 158 high-rise residential, office and corporate buildings that took the breath away from all of her visitors.

The men, or debated "oligarchy," that ran the city over the decades were all alpha male competitive types. They had to be in order to hold the reigns. That being said, if any place had some feature or attraction that they were famous for…the elite of Tampa Bay would always seem to outdo them, paying a fortune to bring in the world's greatest artists to create their own variation of the feature, ten times larger, luxurious and with a dash of flash. A good example of this is the Spinnaker Tower Version 2 that served as lighthouse on the uninhabited island of Shell Key.

Compared to the rest of the country, the collective districts of Tampa Bay posted the highest median household income and the highest employment rate at 88% while the second highest came at 52%, and that city was in a whole nother state. One of the reasons the economy has blossomed so well was due to the largest seaport in the world that was stationed at the mouth of the bay in the district of St. Petersburg. The import/export commercial trade was a booming industry and brought in close to a hundred thousand jobs between the sailors, merchants and longshoremen. And with the advent of the Halo, those workers didn't have to live around St. Petersburg to work at the Port of St. Petersburg.

They had the top ranked football team. The best hockey team. They excelled in almost every watersport invented in the 22nd Century. Actors, singers, celebrities flocked to the city as a platform and second destination to the new Hollywood Hills of San Francisco, and the grandest stage of them all was the city's very own opera hall. The Alero Orchestra Hall was the dream venue for almost every aspiring musician and Broadway actor alive. It was a trademark, known near and far for its massive exterior glass dome that resembled a pearl bulging over the waters of the bay.

On performance nights, the dome turned into a spectacle, a glowing orb of flashing lights, helicopters circling overhead and fireworks lighting up the bay. You didn't have to pay for a ticket to watch the show inside. Civilians, tourists and Tampa natives would simply parked and set up blankets along the beach of the scenic Courtney Campbell Causeway to watch from afar. It was magnificent.

In the heat of the night, the streets of Tampa Bay were always busy with vehicular traffic that never seemed to die down. Pedestrians on foot had evolved to deal with the frost-biting air while making their way to the tourist friendly district of Channelside. This was the heavily patrolled part of the city that contained the three main commercial thoroughfares playing host to diverse array of unique market venders, hole in the wall restaurants, boutiques and shopping malls.

Seminole Time Square was the busiest of the thoroughfares. Dwarfed by skyscrapers in the center of Channelside, people walked the open intersection that was cordoned off to all vehicles. The civilians were always tinted in some color cast by the billboard ads and three enormous TV screens. From Seminole Time Square it was only a short walk to one of the Halo Stations, many theaters, and the ever popular gigantic water fountains of Seminole's Spirit Dream.

Every night, the evening bay news played on all three of the giant TV monitors that took up four floors of the Tampa-Am Financial Building. After that, commercials, promotions and music would fill the streets. Thus, it wasn't uncommon to see massive groups of people just standing in the middle of the intersection watching the news, especially when there were so many dramatic and incredible incidents ensuing with law and order.

At first glance, no one could ever tell the difference that spanned the four years Eliza had been away. No one walked alone. Everyone walked in groups. And when one group was heading towards another, everyone faced forward trying their best not to make eye contact with the strangers. Business owners didn't make small talk with their customers about the weather or chit-chat about any sports team unless they were diehard regulars. Most people just minded his or her own business like always. And the natives knew what streets and districts to stay away from in order to avoid becoming an innocent bystander.

And there were a lot of innocent bystanders...Tampa Bay was a hot bed organized crime. A paradise for those looking to cash in on the seemingly unlimited flow of money to be made in racketeering, extortion, fixed gambling, organ trafficking, narcotics and prostitution just to name a few. Thus war ensued over the territories and headstrong family heads looked to claim dominance. With so much bad blood spilled between warring clans, the police had their hands full not knowing where to start. Tampa consistently posted the highest ratings amongst homicides, forcible rape, aggravated assault, grand theft, cyber fraud, and arson.

Since the fall of the Five Pillars of Minority, the last great faction to oppose the Pierce ten years earlier, Isaac has carved up the city of Tampa Bay to various families and allied clans in order to preserve a pipeline of production and finance. This meant a decrease in the senseless violence, making everyone without a grudge happy. Alberto Pierce, Isaac's eldest son, took the charge in making sure everyone stayed in order while Isaac kept his hands clean running the corporation. The gangs were free to operate within their designated borders and all they had to do was swear an oath of allegiance to the Pierce, paying a 15% tax. A tax everyone referred to as the Bertie, after Alberto. Slang to throw off the police.

After Alberto's death, Isaac figured he had lost enough brothers and sons to the game. So he put his close associate Bosco Rosenberg in charge and entrusted him to run the majority of the Pierce's underground operations in Tampa. The collective, intimidating and highly influential "Rosenberg Association" oversaw activities and collected the Bertie from all of Tampa Bay's gangs. They were given authority to mediate or arbitrate between the other gangs. And there were a lot of mediations. Notable figures within his immediate association included his younger brother Noah as an underboss and the dangerous enforcer, Max Schulberg, aka the "Whisper".

The Winters family headed by the elderly Marlon Winters controlled most of the St. Petersburg district. Since the largest seaport in the empire resided in their district, it was understandable that they'd specialize in grand theft, heists, money laundering and all kinds of trafficking. But they were relatively nonviolent.

Unlike the Winters family, Blade Lee and his so called Ho Sun Dynasty was infamous for coming up with the most inhumane methods for execution. Blade Lee was a vicious criminal who didn't even hesitate to kill his own sons for skimming money in a side game. His Dynasty, predominantly Chinese, controlled the waterfront district of Riverview all the way down to Apollo Beach. This waterfront territory was saturated with a massive colony of shaded boathouses. It stunk and was easy to get lost in. It was hard to patrol without any CCTV cameras, thus human bodies were mostly decayed by the time of their discovery, making it hard to solve any of their murders.

So… since there was so much money to make with little to no police interference, Riverview became sort of a gangster's paradise for the toughest most headstrong bad boys. Thus, rivalries were created when the Ho Sun Dynasty would often drown high-ranking family members in a kill first ask questions later mentality. The districts of Bradenton's Amachi Dojin and Brandon's Vincent Pitt wanted him dead the most. But Rosenberg would never sanction the hit. Blade Lee's reputation of a natural antagonist was a necessary evil to keep his people in line.

Other feuds included the rivalry between neighboring families Mariana Gacha and Kelly Rosetti. Both families have roots in Tampa as deep and historical as the Pierce and Winters, but with their patriarchs passing, the sons have gradually become loose cannons. The mothers, Mariana and Kelly had to step up and take over the reins. Both intransigent entities. Kelly Rosetti held a grudge since Mariana slept with her husband and killed him. But Rosenberg was authorized to pay Rosetti the sum of 3 million to keep her hounds at bay. It's amazing how money soaked with blood can extinguish such a fire.

Some of the more amicable families were the Barreira family who controlled Ybor and East Tampa ran smoothly, and the Kaze-Gumi who operated right smack in the heart of downtown Tampa and Channelside District. Richard Barreira and his family were smooth operators. Everything he did was behind scenes out of the newspapers and off the floor. He even cooperated with the police officers. His men were trained to communicate with the police without dropping any incriminating details. But beneath his charming veneer and reasonable swagger, Richard Barreira was a bonafide sociopath who's killed people for owing less than five bucks.

The Kaze-Gumi of Channelside and the commercial districts of downtown Tampa was run by an elderly old school oyabun named Shinobi Kazemichu. He was once one of the highest yakuza earners for Renji Amaruto based out of Tokyo, Japan. But after a hit on his life left him paralyzed from the waist down, the Pierce took him in as a favor to Amaruto.

Kazemichu's organization was the most financially endowed and envy inducing. All of his men wore the finest designer suits, drove the most expensive cars and lived in the most lavish penthouses. They had to keep a clean and pristine appearance to conduct activity in the face of tourists and the general public. They operated and managed the casinos and high stakes gambling in downtown Tampa. If anyone needed to be taken care of, they had specialized trained enforcers who befriended their victims before luring them away from the public. And as much as almost every family wanted the Kaze-Gumi territory, Kazemichu was well respected not only by the Pierce, Winters, Barreira and his friends back east…he once saved Blade Lee's life when Lee was a youngster scrapping on the streets of Japan. Anyone dumb enough to kill or even hurt Kazemichu was begging to experience every circle of hell.

Those were but a few of the hundreds of gangs, factions and sects operating in Tampa Bay. Everyone knew the cold fact about the American Empire, but most were afraid to just come out and admit it. If there was a godfather of all godfathers, if there was a syndicate and someone or some group that was in charge of it all, Isaac Pierce would be that man. Isaac Pierce was the head of the multi-billion dollar Pierce Conglomerate with hundreds of subsidiaries and partnerships all over the world. And ever since it's acceptance to the Empire's stock exchange, everything has fallen in place for the company. If not by hostile corporate takeovers, then by mere coincidences and accidents that befell their competitors.

It was unbelievable. A diverse family of a mixed race that was once considered minorities in the United States, now in more ways than one, owned the American Empire. And while the talking heads on liberal news outlets would like to credit Isaac's success to his brilliant marketing and ridiculously insightful investments, only a handful of people were aware of Isaac's true source of power. It wasn't in his money or status, but in the influence he had over two weapons. These weapons came in the form of his young nephews who weren't even of drinking age yet.

...

Three armored high-end sports utility vehicles were cruising down the Courtney Campbell Causeway just fifteen minutes till midnight. The orange-yellow tungsten street-lights wiped on and off of their sleek-black metallic coats. The SUVs all traveled at the same pace, one behind the other. With it being so late on a weekday, the convoy faced little to no traffic at all as it sped over the bridge that spanned the icy waters connecting Tampa to Clearwater.

The occupants of the three SUVs were male and female adults dressed in pristine black uniforms that consisted of form-fitting turtleneck shirts with light-shoulder padding under a matching lightweight trench coat. Officially, they were operatives working for a private military firm based out of Orlando called Black Creek Securities. They contracted their services to companies all over the world for protection, infiltration and extraction, and in most cases espionage. Unofficially…They were Isaac's very own private army of syndicate enforcers.

Whilst riding to their destination, they were either brandishing their weapons, polishing their swords and checking their firepower or sitting quietly, meditating about the task at hand. They were also equipped with a Black Creek standardized version of a URM-7 assault rifle that carried forty round thirty-caliber cartridges. But with laws raising ammunition prices after the last world war, 500 round cases were over hundred grand. So each Black Creek soldier was always issued only one magazine per mission.

As per protocol, the vehicle in the middle of the convoy carried the most valuable assets. The driver of the middle vehicle in the convoy was a man named Lazar Malenkov. He was a tall, stout, burly man in his mid-thirties. Aside from his shaved head, roughly trimmed beard and intimidating size, Lazar had kind and gentle looking blue eyes. The kind of eyes that seemed to understand your regrets just before he killed you. Lazar was the youngest of six brothers to Nikita Malenkov, the head of the Russian mafia in the new capital of Volgograd. As a sign of loyalty to the Isaac, Nikita sent Lazar as a provisional hostage ten years ago. Lazar has since proven his dependency as an efficient enforcer within Black Creek and eventually decided to stay by of his own volition.

Sitting beside Lazar in the passenger seat, Adam Park flipped through a digital newspaper on his thin lightweight tablet. Adam was a Korean descendant in his late twenties. He had a dignified look to him, hardly showing any facial expression like an athletic bookworm from an Ivy League school. Usually the architect of such missions, it was rare that Adam was even out in the field. But as a trusted assistant to one of the higher ups, Adam was asked to supervise, only adding to the importance of the mission succeeding without trouble.

In the middle row sat capable enforcers Sean Pierce and Forrest. The two have been best friends since elementary school and gave credence to the phrase, "birds of a feather". With Sean being the godfather's nephew, it didn't take much convincing to have the orphan Forrest go through the training as a fellow enforcer.

Even though Sean was of African-Puerto Rican descent he favored more of his mother's genes with a dark complexion and thick bushy hair that was braided into corn rolls. He was only eighteen-years-old but his tall, slender and edgy appearance made it seem like he was twenty-five. While the standard uniform consisted of the clean black suit and tie, Sean always rebelled, donning his own hip-hop oriented swagger of dark baggy jeans and an oversized padded jacket.

He was wielding his signature twin long barreled semi-automatic chrome-plated pistols. They were gifts from Isaac after Sean successfully completed his first international assassination at the age of sixteen. In that mission, Sean perched himself on the balcony of a hotel that was unfortunately occupied by newlywed couple whose marriage ended abruptly. At 2,275 meters out, Sean used a high-powered scoped rifle to snipe a state senator who was throwing a birthday party for his daughter off the coast of Tampico, Mexico. The yacht was so far away that the police didn't even know where set up a trajectory.

Sean managed this feat before he ever took the Furyx Gene, showing off his natural born ability as a sharpshooter and striking fear in the hearts of the Pierce's enemies. He also showed off his rebellious nature when choosing the codename of Tetra. He could've chosen something hawk or eagle related due to his superb vision. Instead, he chose Tetra after the Mexican Tetra fish. A fish that's said to have no eyes at all.

Being Sean's best friend, Forrest was also able to get away with wearing his own style out on missions. Forrest was also only eighteen, but had a more impressive athletic frame and build than his buddy. Picturesque of his Irish heritage, Forrest had short red spiky hair, sparse freckles and a pale complexion in which normally sported his chiseled muscles by usually wearing very little, despite the harsh cold conditions. Forrest was a crazy individual who reveled in pain. He'd have no qualms in walking the street with nothing but a white tank top, blue jeans and boots.

This goes without saying, that both Sean and Forest were heavily influenced by the ever-prevailing hip-hop culture. And being that no one knew Forrest's last name…His codename was simply Forrest. An arrogant joke aimed towards law enforcement to try and use that against him in the court of law.

Both Sean and Forest were listening to hardcore underground rap on their digital audio players with their ear buds in place. They bobbed their heads, almost in unison as they checked their weapons. Forest's weapon of choice was a pair of twin daggers. The handles were engraved in silver and gold. The blades serrated in a jagged curve. Forest also kept a single handgun tucked in his back for convenient purposes, but his preferred method of operation was to get up close and person with his victims, to get the subtle tingling sensation that spread in his veins when he sank his knife into a person's flesh. And with the Furyx in his veins, Forrest's reputation as the fastest man alive was beginning to grow as he was once clocked sprinting at a staggering 48mph. The only man said to be faster was sitting right behind him.

In the back row, twenty-year-old Braden Pierce was lying on his back stretched over the seats, smoking a cigarette with his nostalgic gaze peering through the windows at the lampposts that flashed by. Like his brother, Braden was mixed, but favored more of his father's Puerto Rican genes. He had short wavy hair with sharp thin sideburns that came down to the edge of his jaw line. His trimmed, barely-there mustache and naturally defiant brown eyes always made him a figure of authority as soon as he stepped in a room. The bronze complexion of his skin carried multiple uneven hues.

Standing at six foot two, Braden was built like a professional baseball player with long legs and chiseled forearms. Unlike his younger brother, Braden didn't mind wearing the black suit and turtleneck, but also wore black leather manufactured gloves that were resistant to heat, cold, or electricity.

The only weapon Braden ever needed was resting on his chest with the handle propped just beneath his chin. His long samurai katana sword was a Masahiro blade. The foot-long handle or tsuka was wrapped in a black cotton cloth. The blade that rested inside the black lacquer sheath was twenty-seven inches long, razor sharp, and tested to withstand the impact of most fifty-caliber bullets. Braden went by the code name of Mako after his favorite animal.

Braden didn't blink. With his sharp mind and Furyx, he was able to count and remember the number of lampposts that flashed by. Playing such mental games was his way of keeping his mind preoccupied from thinking about anything else. He wasn't a chain smoker. He wasn't even a casual smoker. He wasn't addicted and he didn't smoke to fit in. The nicotine simply calmed him down. It was going on his fifth year of service with Black Creek, and even still…the exciting anticipation of combat was hard to contain.

"Ah, shit man." Adam whispered to himself.

. For most of the ride over all you could hear was the smooth hum of the engine and mechanical clanks of Sean playing with his pistol. Now that they were less than five minutes till reaching their destination, Adam's voice rung out and captured Lazar's attention. Adam wasn't the frustrated easily annoyed type. Even on missions or in heated arguments, he hardly ever raised his voice and always spoke in a calm casual tone as if nothing could ever be so serious.

"Can you believe this? The police arrested yet another asshole claiming to be Braden Pierce. They shot him after trying to rob a Fuel-and-Go off of Hillsborough and Webb. Yep…He's dead. Tax money hard at work. Thanks boys." Adam said casually as he read off of his tablet.

Lazar chuckled to himself as he shook his head in disbelief. He passed a glance into the rearview mirror but Braden was still lying down out of sight.

"Find this amusing, do you Lazar? The press is making Braden out to look like this Jesse James figure." Adam added.

"Jesse James? Who's that then?" Lazar asked in his watered down Russian accent.

Adam scoffed. "It doesn't matter. The point is this is press we don't need. We're going to need Rosenberg to send a message through the ranks. People need to keep their mouths shut. And you guys…"

Adam turned around to check on Forest and Sean. Both were done with their preparations and resting their eyes. "Hey. Hey. What the hell you guys think you're doing? Taking a nap?" Adam called out lightly.

Forrest was the first to open his eyes, furrowing his eyebrows as Adam reached back to poke at Sean. The gaze cast by Forrest was a warning. None of the enforcers liked to be touched, but they were almost about to arrive. For some reason, Adam liked to skate on thin ice to see how much he could get away with the young men.

"Easy eh? The boys have been up for six straight days. It's a miracle we made it back here in time." Lazar beseeched him.

"Yeah, well that's what that Furyx is for. We must have spent over a million bucks to get them juiced up." Adam reminded.

"Yeah and that shit almost got us killed." Sean uttered in a laid back slur.

"I know right. I'd love to see you try it. Whether he lives or not, I just want to see him go through the shakes." Forrest said before bobbing his own shoulders with a malicious smirk.

Sean laughed a laugh of approval towards his friend's joke before raising an eyebrow at Adam. "What you wake us for?"

"We're almost there. I need you guys to get your head straight. Braden up back there?" Adam asked.

Forrest turned around. Braden's eyes were still looking out the window with a stoic expression. Forest chuckled to himself. "Yeah, he up. Looking like he's wondering why the earth rotates, like always."

Sean looked over his shoulder to his older brother. "You good?"

"I'm fine. Give your gun." Braden told him in a low apathetic tone.

Sean grinned as he handed Braden one of his loaded pistols. "Every time man. This is like the hundredth flipping time, and he still asks to check my guns. It's not like they gonna have guns."

"No tellin what they'll be draggin along, boys." Lazar uttered.

"*I* know what they'll be draggin along." Adam haughtily chimed in.

He then synched his tablet up with the SUV's dashboard's wireless connection. This allowed him to display his tablet screen on to every window in the vehicle save for the driver's windshield. You couldn't see the exact image because the government thought that would be too dangerous. Instead, there was a red laser outline of images, text and data, allowing passengers to see out of the window transparently through the projections. It allowed Adam to illustrate what he was talking about, even though they should've paid attention during their mission brief.

"The target is Eduardo Salazar. A Columbian cocaine supplier foolish enough to conspire with Hollandale and Holmes behind our backs. His flight is scheduled to take off in less than fifteen. His men are cartel men born and bred, most likely armed with knock off assault rifles and Spanish rapiers. Where they come from, it isn't uncommon to see public executions and abductions. They don't value human lives all too highly. And they know that retreating today means certain death tomorrow. That being said, you can expect quite a fight."

Forrest and Sean nodded before Sean received a light tap on his shoulder. Braden was returning the pistol.

"Was it good? Did I load it to your standards and qualifications?" Sean mocked, mispronouncing qualifications.

"Killing Salazar shouldn't be too difficult. It's the man guarding him who may make things difficult. A Spanish mercenary named Tulio." Adam said.

"Torreto? Tulio Torreto?" Lazar asked.

"You've heard of this Tulio Torreto, but not Jesse James? What the hell, Lazar?" Adam asked lightheartedly with a smirk.

"We've all heard of Tulio. The dude's a behemoth." Forrest mentioned.

"Yeah, well that behemoth has the Furyx Gene in him. He's also a prized bullfighter in his homeland. The bastard's been killing bulls with his bare hands. Can't believe they still even have bullfighting." Adam said.

"So he's the real deal then?" Forrest said.

"Mmhmm.." Adam uttered.

"Oye, Maki!" Lazar called back with a grin. "Did you hear what Adam here was telling me? They caught another one pretending to be you."

Lazar's taunt amused Sean and Forrest who both knew that Braden wasn't one who thrived on attention. In fact, Braden despised it. In the five years Braden has been out in the field pulling off daring assassinations and executing business deals and negotiations, not a single photograph has been taken of him despite Tampa Bay being one of the most watched cities in the world. It was only his marquee name that's been dropped here and there.

Adam grinned. "You know this is the sort of thing that keeps David up at night."

"I don't give a damn." Sean declared with obvious animosity.

"I know right. Is there anything that doesn't keep him up? You know. Besides Japanese porno?" Forrest chimed in.

"Gross… You should care, Sean. We all should care." Adam said as he put his computer tablet in a slot on his door. "Old man Isaac isn't going be around forever. David will be the next head, sooner or later."

"Whatever." Sean uttered.

"Oye Oye! What you got against David, eh?" Lazar asked him.

"You know why! I just don't trust him. He's all dollars and cents. I never seen him do any of these missions or get his hands dirty not once! But he stands there and gives out these orders like he's fucking Napoleon. He doesn't give a damn about collateral damage or casualties on our side. As long as we make it happen. How can I respect a punk like that?"

Agreeing with Sean yet lacking the gumption to speak out, Lazar and Forrest simply chuckled with a nod. After a brief moment of silence, Adam spoke up. "In any case…Please don't do anything too reckless. We need to get this done but we need to keep it tight and clean. Conquer and retreat. Salazar is the primary objective."

Braden sighed with a mystic look of boredom. His eyes followed the stars and noted their rotation as the vehicle curved smoothly through several turns. Finally sitting up and propping his sword to stand between his legs, Braden took in a deep breath and closed his eyes.

"Sean..." Braden started in a calm yet stern tone. For some reason everyone sensed that Braden had something important to say and gave him their full attention.

"You should not speak ill of David. He may have his vices and flaws just like the next man, but he is still our cousin and the son of the chief. None of us can ever begin to fathom how it must feel to lose all six of his older brothers in the span of one decade. The sadness. The antipathy. We should consider this when coming to our own rash judgments on his character. And simply trust in his."

Forrest and Sean nodded, slightly feeling the shame of speaking out against David although they'd never admit it. Lazar wore a proud grin as he followed the lead vehicle onto the exit that led directly to the Clearwater airstrip. From the higher view from the ramp off of the causeway, Adam could see the hangers out in the distance and noticed that the relatively small one-story airport was unusually well lit for that time at night. Rows of limousines were parked in the terminal drop off point with no one bothering to park them in the garage. Adam discerned that the Colombians knew they were in danger and probably set the flood lights up to avoid a surprise ambush.

Adam and Lazar exchanged glances, both acknowledging what they had to do. Adam pressed a button on the dashboard computer screen to turn on his communicator to the other vehicles. "Alright ladies and gentlemen. They're ready for us. A tactical stealth approach is unlikely. Lead vehicle, punch it. We ram through and take out anyone stupid enough not to run away. Over."

After two quick confirmations from the other vehicles came in, the SUVs increased their acceleration to 80 mph as they approached the first gated checkpoint. As ordered, the lead vehicle crashed through the aluminum gates and set off the facility's alarm system. In an exaggerated comical fashion, Sean and Forrest were getting amped up by rocking back and forth in their chairs, shaking their heads wildly with wide grins on their faces.

Braden finally opened his eyes. The stoic look of boredom that was once there had completely disappeared. In its place was a haunting grin of a bloodthirsty competitor ready to be let out of the gate. Grasping the handle of his long katana, Braden's Furyx induced hearing honed in on the sounds coming from four hundred meters out. They were the sounds of about thirty hurried footsteps running with aggression in their strides.

"Lazar! Lose the roof." Braden ordered.

Lazar shot an absurd look through the rearview mirror at Braden. "Are you crazy? It's colder than a yeti's balls out here! At least wait till we get through the electrical fences!"

Sean and Forest laughed at Lazar's uncharacteristic fear of pain. Even Adam couldn't help but smirk in amusement towards the zeal of the young men. It was as if they were on their way to an amusement park, completely unprofessional, and yet with proven track record of success! Within seconds of the alarm being sounded, the lead SUV had the vehicles crashing through the glass entrance of lobby and scrubbing rubber down the slick marble floors of the concourse walkway.

Airport staff was light, and there were only a handful of security guards roaming around. Most were paid off by the Columbians to keep quiet so the Black Creek didn't worry about lost sleep for mowing down anyone who was too slow to move out of the way.

As Adam predicted, the Columbians in Hanger 3 were armed with cheap assault rifles and Spanish rapiers. They hurried to move their boss from his limo to the private jet that was parked nearby. Despite Eduardo Salazar being in his late fifties, he was still a healthy capable man. The stylish streaks of white in his short black hair distinguished him amongst his colleagues. The lead bodyguard dragging him by the arm was Tulio Torreto. The large six foot five Spanish native's appearance lived up to the hype and lent credibility to the rumors of his barehanded bullfighting days. The cartel members all wore some variety of dark silk designer shirts over their electronically heated tank tops, suggesting that their warning to get out of dodge was short notice.

Just as Tulio and Salazar were reaching the steps of their private jet, the black SUVs came crashing out of a terminal's waiting room and onto the runway, speeding towards the hangers.

"Hurry, Roberto! Start the plane." Salazar shouted to his pilot as he hurried into the cabin. Tulio and three other Columbian accountants followed Salazar on board before Tulio closed the door.

"Damn it! Lose the top, Lazar!" Braden shouted from the backseat of the SUV. "Put it in autopilot if you're afraid of your precious truck."

"All right you crazy bastard!" Lazar shouted angrily.

With the push of a button, Lazar ejected the rooftop and sent it flying off with the velocity of the wind. He watched as Braden removed his dark trench coat and leaned forward in the aisle between Forest and Sean. "Oye! At least wait until I stop, Braden!" Lazar shouted.

It was too late. As soon as the SUV was within fifty feet of the nearest cartel member, Braden pushed off the backseat to launch himself into the air, draw his katana and use the force of his landing to sink the razor sharp blade through a man's left shoulder, severing his aorta and dislodging his lunge all in one swing. The sight of first blood sent an uncontainable grin of malicious satisfaction over Braden as the man collapsed like a broken android.

"Stop the cars. Get out there and terrorize, kids. Let's move!" Adam ordered through the communicator in his usual calm unnerving tone.

All at once, the SUVs came to a screeching halt in stylish synchronized fashion. The Black Creek moved silently without a shred of anxiety or caution. It was routine as if every single soldier, male and female, had gone through the same mission over a hundred times. The enemy cartel soldiers boldly engaged them, keeping in mind that the elite Black Creek were still only humans. Some opened fire. Some drew their swords.

The private jet emerged from the hanger and rolled onto the runway. With the sounds of popping gun shots ringing out, Salazar nervously crawled over to a window seat and peered out. A panic attack was setting in as he witnessed Braden taking on a group of four cartel members. Two of them had guns, the other two ran forward with their rapiers in hand. Using the shadows of blind spots in the flood light coverage, Braden managed evade the line of automatic fire, close in, and cut them down, one strike each. Salazar watched in horror as his men fingered at the bloody gorges on their chest and neck area, each of them screaming in pain and agony as they fell to the tarmac.

"Oh my god. Is that him? Is that Braden Pierce?" Salazar asked Tulio.

The more battle-hardened Tulio bent over from his position in the aisle walkway to look out the window. A growling sigh exhale was released as he shook his head. "Si. That's him alright. One can never forget that lack of empathy."

A lack of human emotion was one way to describe Braden in the heat of battle. He didn't take narcotics or hallucinations. He didn't smoke weed like his brother or lust for sex as furiously as Lazar. Combat was Braden's high. With most people, they'd have to warm themselves up to get into the zone. From the moment Braden drew his sword he lost himself from any sense of reality in space or time. He didn't think about consequences or even his own safety. The only thing that concerned him was that which was in front of him. Anyone caught in his crosshairs became the target. It was nine Black Creek operatives against thirty. But if you were to tell someone that Braden was involved, they'd call it asymmetrical warfare that favored Black Creek.

Well trained in the Shiranui-ryu style of swordsmanship, Braden showed why he was in a league of his own. Even without the Furyx, Braden's strikes were always swift, accurate and intentional. He barely used his sword to parry or clang at their blades. Braden's gifted agility and expert footwork gave him the ability to alter his eye level and move from the front of his opponents to the side and behind them within a blink of the eye. The Furyx only added strength and speed to his offense. One cut from Braden severed bones and ripped through ballistic armor like chopping through a biscuit. Other than Braden, Sean, Forrest, and Tulio, no one else in the battle had Furyx in their system.

Sean and Forrest were usually together in battle. Sean stood at a safe distance from enemies while picking them off one by one with his pistols. Anyone who attempted to get too close to Sean was stabbed half a dozen times before crumbling to the ground. Forrest had lightning quick reflexes and displayed an impressive array of quick short-range strikes with his daggers. Sean provided the long range projectile attack. Forrest got up close and personal.

Lazar didn't participate in the fighting but stood next to the vehicle overseeing the fight. Adam was also still sitting casually inside the vehicle while the frantic skirmish waged on. He was supposed to keep tabs that each man was doing what they were paid well to do. But that task seemed unnecessary. Compared to the Black Creek, the cartel enforcers were like middle school students defending a group of high school seniors.

Suddenly, the flash of red and blue lights reflecting off of the side mirror caught his eye. First responders from the Clearwater District Police Agency had arrived but it was sooner than expected. Someone must have tipped them off and the revelation bothered Adam. He knew the police would be arriving but not so quickly and not with their SWAT team.

"Fellas, we got company. 5-O at your six. 5-O at your six. Sean, light their asses up." Adam said casually, knowing the Furyx users would hear his words.

Just as he yanked his steel from a man's sternum, Braden turned around to see three patrol cars and a SWAT van approaching. Sean stopped firing his guns to shoot a mocking smile towards his older brother. He knew Braden had an overwhelming abhorrence for law enforcement. It was so bad that he had jeopardized several missions in the past just to kill trivial deputies who were getting away.

Sean taunted with glee. "You can't have them both!"

A glare of frustration surfaced as Braden realized that Sean was right. The jet was making the first of its four turns to ascend on the runway. The very appearance of the police arriving as if they had the authority and power to stop him was beyond insulting. As much as he wanted to slay each and every cop who dared step out of their cars, he could never forgive himself if Salazar got away due to his selfishness. Thus, he clenched his teeth and returned the sword to his sheath. After taking in a deep breath, he lowered himself into a squat and broke out in a full sprint towards the jet.

With a smirk on his face, Sean turned to face the patrol cars. He held up and aimed his twin long-barreled pistols at them. His eye pupils contracted as his Furyx vision zoomed in on the closest sedan 250 yards out. After a moment's hesitation, Sean pulled both triggers at once, sending two armor piercing bullets whistling through the wind.

One bullet pierced through a car's windshield and hit the driver square between the eyes, killing him instantly. Before the man in the passenger seat could reach for the steering wheel, the car clipped a parked baggage carrier and popped into the air flipping upside down onto the roof. The other bullet scraped through the door panel of a second and hit the axle near the left rear tire. The car ended up fishtailing sideways before barrel rolling onto the grassy runway infield.

Seeing what just happened, the last squad car radioed for the SWAT van to stop immediately and pursue on foot. After coming to a screeching halt armored police officers filed out with their government issued riot shields, assault rifles and an assortment of high voltage weaponry.

Most of the SWAT team ran towards the fray with their own stun batons. But two specialists grabbed Voltyankers that were as large as rocket launchers. The two officers ran to within forty feet of the nearest criminal, got down on one knee, and fired the Voltyankers with a blunt deafening boom. Thick electrical charged cable nets shot forward and wrapped up two cartel members, sending the state restricted 10,000 volts through their bodies before dropping them. The officers would then retract the nets and reel in their catch.

Forrest heard the sounds of the Voltyankers and turned around to see what just happened. "Shit man! We need to go!" He shouted.

"Hold ya ground, boy! I say when it's time to go! Keep your position and hold them off."

Sean words strengthen the resolve of the other Black Creek soldiers. Everyone nodded and continued engaging both the Colombians and SWAT team. Braden was still printing across the landing zone. Salazar watched in horror as Braden closed in on the plane like a cheetah hunting a gazelle.

"Roberto! Speed this thing up!" Salazar screamed.

It wouldn't do any good. Braden caught up to the plane and leaped to claw his hands onto the left wing. Tulio saw him. After whipping up his gold-handled bullfighting sword, he headed for the plane's emergency exit. The sounds of Braden climbing to the top of the cabin made Salazar trembled viciously. Just as Tulio opened the exit door, Braden's blade struck through the roof ceiling causing Salazar to scream like a woman.

With icy wind blowing in his face, Braden used both hands to carve his sword through the roof of the cabin. "That's far enough, my friend!" Tulio shouted.

Braden squinted into the gust to see the dark cast of Tulio standing seven feet away with his sword at the ready. With one hand, Tulio unbuttoned his black collared shirt and took it off. A fiery bull tattooed across his bulky chest. Braden's eagle eyes stayed focused on the matador as he slowly pulled his sword out of the plane and rose from his knees.

"It's a shame. So young. So much potential. Could have accomplished so much." Tulio said in a condescending tone over the roar of the engines.

Without any words of his own, Braden casually approached Tulio as the plane entered it's third of four turns. Quick as a spark, Braden started the intense swordfight with a quick thrust aimed for Tulio's throat. Tulio easily parried the blow and flicked his wrist to return swing for Braden's throat. Braden instinctively leaned back to evade the strike while raising his sword for another swing of his own.

While Tulio was much stronger, Braden quickly found a weakness and used it against him. Tulio's weakness was his dependency on the quick forward thrusts, naturally in the style of delivering deathblows to the bull's neck. To Braden, it was all too predictable. Blocking Tulio's sword, Braden would frustrate him by countering with his own quick jabs to the face.

The jet finally turned onto its last stretch of the runway. Just as Braden and Tulio locked swords, the jet began to pick up speed. Tulio used the momentum of the thrusts to shove Braden on his back. Sliding toward the tail end of the jet, Braden struggled to regain control and eventually came to a halt while lying on his belly. The jet gave another thrust forward. The force of this thrust caused Tulio to lose his footing and stumble forward toward Braden. Before Tulio could regain his posture, Braden sprang forward and swung upward, slicing his sword across Tulio's chest and sending him spiraling off the plane.

The plane was picking up speed and his target still alive and well. Braden crouched down to avoid sliding off and scrambled to make a decision. His time was running out. Adrenaline driven instincts kicked in. Just as the front wheels lifted off the ground, Braden pushed forward and leaped towards the right wing. With both hands tightly wound around the handle, Braden raised his sword as far back over his head as it could go and gathered all of his strength to swing the blade downward. The force of his swing in midair caused Braden to do a front flip as the razor sharp katana severed through several layers of steel and fiberglass to detach the wing.

…

Seconds later, Braden hit the ground hard and tumbled hard with knee-breaking momentum before landing face forward on his chest. Despite the back padding of his turtleneck being torn to shreds, Braden still managed to keep a grip his sword in one hand. It took him a moment of lying on the rough, grainy tarmac before he began to pick himself up. He had minor scrapes over his shoulder blades and the soreness in his neck was starting to kick in, but that was it.

With his heart still racing, he patted the dirt off of the front of his pants and looked around for his sword scabbard that came loose during the tumble. He found it and reattached it to the belt latch on his waist. Just as he was casually returning the sword to his sheath, Salazar's plane crashed down in a hellish explosion over 400 yards away. The sound of the impact had no effect on Braden. He didn't even care to see how high the fireball rose into the air.

No…Braden's job was done and he pulled it off in a marvelous fashion that would eventually become his trademark. And yet, Braden's attention was focused elsewhere. He prided himself in not only completing his tasks no matter how difficult the challenge, but also on his stealth and ability to avoid detection and pursuit. As an enforcer, Braden had gotten comfortable doing the pursuing. But for the ninth straight mission in six months, Braden noticed that someone was watching him.

Back towards the airport's main building, he saw the silhouette figure of a man standing on the roof's ledge. Even with his Furyx vision, it was difficult from Braden's position to clearly see the person's face at night. But he knew it was the same person as before. His mysterious follower had the same excessive use of an aqua-scented cologne. The thing that pissed Braden off the most was the cavalier sense that his secret admirer let off. Judging by the silhouette, the figure had long hair and a loose fitted coat, both of which blew in the wind like he or she was some kind superior being.

Lazar drove up with the convertible SUV as Braden stood focused on the mysterious figure, hoping to get a clear view of their face. Adam, Sean and Forrest were already strapped inside. Sean and Forrest in particular were both sprawled out in their seats, exhausted and overworked. The cartel had put up quite a fight. If the syndicate had used any other gang, Salazar might have lived. Forrest's white tank top had several tears in it suggesting he received several hacks by long fast-whipping Spanish rapiers. Even Sean was trying to regain control of his trembling fingertips. It was rare but several officers actually managed to Taser Sean more than once.

Adam examined the fiery wreck and could hear the emergency vehicles blaring in the distance. "We need to get out of here." He said with disappointment.

Braden approached Sean and yanked at him while extending his finger towards the mysterious figure. "Tetra. Tell me you see that man. Do you see him?"

Groggy and in a daze, Sean rolled his head to focus in on the direction Braden was pointing in. Noticing Sean's confused expression, Braden turned back to the airport. Even he could see that the figure was no longer there.

"Nah bruh. Should I? What am I supposed to be looking for?" Sean asked as he covered his face, no longer wanting to see any more lights.

Braden scoffed with annoyance. "Never mind. It's nothing." Braden grabbed the top frame of the roofless SUV and swung himself into the backseat.

"Yeah. I hope you're happy, you truculent prick." Lazar complained as he drove off. "I've had this truck for a whole five months. It was a new record for me. But no. You had to go and fuck it up. Hasty arse!"

Lazar's complaining alleviated Sean and Forrest's pain as they found his attitude more than amusing. Adam rolled his eyes as he lit up a cigarette. "This transport is the last thing we should concern ourselves with gentlemen. It's best we let me explain things to David."

"Aye. He's all yours." Lazar agreed.

In the backseat, Braden continued to peer towards the airport that was fading in the distance. There was something extremely ominous and foreboding about the figure. The fact that the same man or woman could have kept tabs on him for so long… To Braden, it meant that this figure was nothing to take lightly. It could turn out to be a thorn in his side.

Chapter 8: Press and Private Investigators

"How's my hair?"

Michelle Hausermann stood in front of her lesbian camerawoman with the chaotic night crime scene of the Clearwater airport for her backdrop. Firemen ran pumping water from the bay to wrestle the flames of the destroyed aircraft. A helicopter hovered overhead with spotlights searching for any movement of survivors trying to escape. Police had a perimeter of the crime scene cordoned off. And over thirty different news station and online media outlets swarmed to get answers and take pictures, questioning everyone from injured cartel men and to the janitors slaving to clean up the facilities before dawn.

"Your hair's good Michelle. Can we get this and get out of here?" Ali asked as she hoisted the camera up on her shoulder.

"Alright, okay." Michelle said, putting on her "happy face" and straightening out her beige suit jacket. "This is Michelle Hausermann, reporting from Channel 6B. As you can see, the hardworking men and women of the CD fire department are still fighting the flames of what appears to be yet another mafia related attack. Amongst the seventeen dead and eight injured, reports indicate that one fatality is millionaire Columbian nationalist and alleged drug trafficker, Eduardo Salazar."

She continued. "Salazar was the majority shareholder of KamiNet Industries. A company that specializes in both electronics and data production. It was rumored that KamiNet, which is based out of New Orleans, was also fierce competitor of Japanese powerhouse Tsukishima Industries. While Tsukishima's main offices are located in Tokyo, it's well known that they share their U.S. offices with the Pierce Corporation in downtown Tampa."

"Is it just a coincidence? That's not up for me to say. No doubt the illustrious Pierce Corp already has a PR team hard at work conjuring up a number of plausible explanations. We look forward to seeing what they come up with. I'm Michelle Hausermann of 6B Action news, reporting from the Clearwater district. We'll be staying on the scene all night to keep you apprised of any updates. Back to you, Allen." Michelle said to wrap up.

"Michelle! Are you serious? I have to pick Maddie up at six. Ashlyn doesn't get home until eight!" Ali complained after stopping the recording.

"We have to stay, Ali. Look around! This has the stink of Pierce written all over it. Reminds you of the Five Pillar days when the financial building burned down. Something big is going to happen. And we need to be in front of it." Michelle told her with certainty.

Just then, Michelle caught sight of a gold luxury sedan approaching the scene. Dimples appeared in her cheeks as she smiled. "Oh. And speak of the devil. Here comes my man."

Michelle was an inquisitive Caucasian brunette in her late thirties. She had eloquent voice and possessed a killer body that was blessed with a broad set. Despite escaping the clutches of near-death "accidents" on several occasions, she was never swayed her from spitting out her honest thoughts on the most incriminating scandals and blatant evidence of corruption. The man arriving in a gold sedan was a man she had been romantically linked to on-and-off for almost seven years.

Now at the rank of Inspector Detective, Angel Gazi parked a good distance away from the tape and exited the vehicle with the glossy gaze of someone who wasn't looking forward to so early a start to the day. Clouds were moving in which meant more wind and more cold. Still dressed sharply despite his meager salary, Gazi now had a vertical scar no larger than the diameter of a dime under his right eye. He was stabbed in the face two years earlier from a botched contract hit.

The seasoned vet looked around, taking in the light tint of burning fuel. He wasn't the only detective on site. There were high ranking officers from the six neighboring districts of Clearwater. Gazi was stationed in the heart of Tampa. He was called out due to a tip that one of his long-standing suspects was involved in the fray. And yet, despite the busy congested crime scene where no doubt evidence contamination was inevitable, Michelle Hausermann's haughty smile of satisfaction was the first thing to get his attention. Several investigators approached to fill him in. After hearing the brief, Gazi let the officers escort him through the wave of reporters, each sticking a recording device in his face, fire-hosing him with a number of questions.

"This is a mess." Gazi uttered under the decibel level of barking questions and accusations.

He spotted several uniformed officers speaking with several soldierly looking gentlemen in thick rubber work overalls and heavy duty gloves. Gazi deduced that they must have worked at the local fish processing plant off of 49th Street. Irish mob boss, Dorsey McLean's men. Detective Gazi yanked the nearest officer closer and growled for him to get those unis' away from McLean's men. With an uneasy look, the officer agreed. Officer Dikowski was a native to the area. He knew McLean was paid up so getting his men to back away wouldn't be an easy task.

Michelle branched out from the cluster and followed him with Ali struggling to keep up with her. "Inspector Gazi. Inspector Gazi." She called out.

Gazi ignored her as he lifted the cordoning tape and entered the perimeter. Angered, Michelle quickly lifted the tape and rushed past the barricade of officers who were too slow to catch her. With Ali stuck back at the line, Michelle pulled out her pen that seconded as a covert digital audio recorder.

She shouted, "Angel!"

Gazi stopped with the two young officers who were escorting him. He gestured for them to go on without him. Then he turned to her and made no attempt to hide a grimace of obvious agitation. With his hands in his pockets, his jacket waving in the soft, yet frigid gust, he watched the unwavering lop-sided grin curl up on her face.

"Evening, Angel. I see your legend has kicked up quite a storm tonight." Michelle sneered.

"Ask your questions woman." Gazi said sternly. The tone of his voice had gotten deeper and coarser over the years, more than likely from the stress and anxiety.

"Fine then." Michelle said as she wiped off her grin for a more serious look. She turned on her recorded with a twist of the pen.

"I think what everyone is wondering is what the police intend on doing about the rising crime in the city. For the sixth time this month, we have yet again, another open act of violence committed by what appears to be predicated between feuding clans of organized crime. Even with guns supposedly outlawed, we still see gun casings and officers shot by assault rifles. Now I'm no detective, but if I can see where all roads lead to, why can't you? Or are the local and state police just unfit to handle the situation?" Michelle asked him with complete journalistic integrity.

Gazi closed his eyes with a clench of the jaw. He knew very well that each question was double edged, designed for disaster no matter what the answer was.

"You think this a job best left up to the Imperial Government?" He began. "Maybe if the mayor wasn't so busy playing golf with the likes of Boss Rosenberg and David Pierce, they'd have a more enthusiastic approach."

"So you are admitting that Boss Rosenberg and David Pierce are involved in some way to these slayings? If not! If not involved, there is at the very least some connection, right?" Michelle asked.

Gazi shook his head. "Nothing further, Michelle. I have people waiting." Gazi said before gesturing for the closest deputy to come and escort her back behind the lines.

Michelle shot Gazi a look as if to say, "Come on Angel, don't be like that." And Gazi responded with his own look that seemed to say, "Bitch please."

James Slater was a young athletic SWAT member with short black hair and brown eyes. He was sitting in the back of an ambulance receiving treatment for shoulder wound from one of Sean's pistols. Even though Slater had managed to nab a cartel member using the Voltyankers, he didn't feel proud or accomplished. The throbbing pain in his shoulder was nothing compared to the burning unrest from losing his fellow officers. Gazi approached him.

"Slater. You still alive?" Gazi joked with a serious tone. It was Gazi's first time meeting Slater, but Gazi always talked to people as if he's known them for years. The helicopter was hovering overhead just now. Gazi waved it away, annoyed from the bright light. Slater nodded with a forced smile as a humanoid paramedic stuck a needle of morphine below the wound close to his armpit.

"Any casualties on our side?" Gazi asked.

"Sproles and Derrickson, sir." Slater told him.

Gazi nodded sympathetically. "So it was Salazar then?"

Slater used the back of his gloved hand to wipe the sweat from his forehead. "Don't know. By time we arrived, the plane was already in motion. Saw someone sprinting towards it. The guy was so freaking fast. I couldn't believe it."

"Was it Braden Pierce?" Gazi asked with high hopes and anticipation.

Hating to have to disappoint, Slater shook his head no. "I couldn't see, sir. He was moving so fast and it was so fuckin dark. Everyone was using code names like Tetris and Marko."

"Damn!" Gazi exclaimed.

"Sorry sir. We did the best we could. But these guys were so stacked with heat. I'm telling you they weren't some random gang off the streets. These guys had to be mercs or some kind of Special Forces." Slater told him.

Just then, Gazi caught sight of someone standing in the shadows under a jet way. The figure had long hair and a dark trench coat that blew with the wind. The only reason Gazi was able to spot him was from the single spark that came from lighting a cigarette.

Gazi patted Slater on the good side of his back. "Don't worry soldier. Rest up. I'll look into getting you promoted to my division."

Gazi began walking off toward the jet way as Slater rolled his eyes with skepticism. Fortunately, Gazi didn't see it. With so much of the investigation still underway, Gazi was able to walk to the suspicious character under the dark shade of the jet way without drawing too much attention. Only Michelle Hausermann noticed Gazi skulking off, but chose to watch them from a distance and possibly tail Gazi's contact after they separated.

"Evening. Let me guess. You saw the whole thing. Who was on the plane?" Gazi started.

Gavin Hassel raised his hand slowly to tuck his long healthy bangs behind his right ear. He took in a deep puff of his cigarette and answered in his usual apathetic tone. "Colombia's favorite son. It was a solid hit. The syndicate came with the sole purpose of ending lives tonight."

Gavin was now twenty-four years old. He still wore his hair long. He still carried his long Claymore sword on his back and he still wore a long cloak-like dark trench coat. Only now, his trench coats were more expensive and he had several kinds, all designer brands. He had gotten taller, now standing six foot four. He already had good hygiene, but he was now enriched with cologne and wore expensive jewelry like silver earrings and a gem-crusted pendant necklace. Even his French imported cigarettes cost fifty dollars a pack. But he could afford everything. Being a private investigator with super human senses could make a man very valuable.

"Did you see Braden? Did you see his face clearly?" Gazi asked.

"Absolutely." Gavin told him.

Gazi looked up to the sky with wonder. "Oh my god. So it's true. All the rumors about him being some kind of…" Gazi stopped himself.

Gavin nodded, understanding the detective's sentiment. "His heart beats louder than most. The kid's reckless and getting much bolder. He was on the plane before it crashed and walked away from it like it was a fall from a swing set. It's chilling how someone so young can be so cold, unaffected. There's definitely something wrong with that one." Gavin shared.

Gavin watched as Gazi paced close to a wall, distraught with stress. Gavin couldn't understand what he was so worried about. "Detective. I saw his face. Arrest him. I'll testify."

Gazi groaned. "Yeah. I'll do that, and old man Isaac will have his cult of lawyers strut in with a trombone up their ass and drill you with questions about how you were able to clearly see him cut down a plane during takeoff in the middle of the night. And mind you, a jury of your peers still hasn't even heard of the Furyx Gene. Hell, even I've only heard rumors."

Gavin wondered to himself. "Then let me investigate him. I'll find you conclusive evidence. Pro bono."

Gazi nodded, mentally trying to keep himself above the waters of shame. "Don't get yourself killed, Gavin. You're much too young to die for nothing."

Gavin let out a tension breaking smirk before turning to walk off. "Trust me, detective. Everything I do is for a reason. Even if it makes sense to only me."

The impressive skyline of illuminated buildings that landmarked the city were all mostly centered around busy area of downtown Tampa, mainly in the districts of Ybor, Channelside, Hyde Park and Davis Island. Amongst the skyscrapers of financial institutes and corporate buildings were two giant monoliths. The world famous Pierce Luxury Hotel of Tampa and the corporate office building of the Pierce Corporation.

The Pierce Luxury Hotels were amazing attractions placed in every major city all over the world. With Tampa Bay's Pierce Hotel being the first of the five-star chains, it was a flagship masterpiece that housed over 6,000 rooms within 35 floors in a building that was as massive as a football superdome stadium. The hotel was known for its white royally gothic architecture and medieval dragon designs.

Entering the hotel and into the lobby was like walking into a new dimension. The walls were paved in a white lustful gloss that showcased a number of romantic and neoclassic paintings that were each worth a fortune in of itself. The warm air scented with vanilla would hit you as your attention was captured by an elaborate neoclassical white marble fountain in the center of the open space. Large clear crystal chandeliers hung down from the high vaulted ceilings in an exquisite design.

Red plush carpet held you firm as you would be escorted by a number of properly groomed attractive concierges who were trained to treat each and every guest as a king or queen. The hotel's atrium was breathtaking. So breathtaking that the guests forwent use of the elevators specifically to ride the spiral escalators around the atrium and take in its magnificent view.

The wide-open space of the rotunda surrounded the world's highest indoor water fountain. The base of this fountain was a large white marble pool the size of a hockey rink. Emerging from the pool was a 68 foot golden Chinese Dragon that flew upward with its talons reaching for the glass ceiling. Mists sprayed sporadically from under its scales while a geyser of red LED lit water shot from the dragon's mouth and hit a clear ceramic umbrella causing a rain to fall back down into the pool without a single drop hitting the guests or the carpet.

The hotel was lined with cameras, scanners, and over a hundred salary paid undercover Black Creek operatives who would blend in with the guests as tourists. With anyone perceived to be a threat, agents were granted permission to intercept and detain without question.

Each hotel around the world had its own unique special feature amongst the standard casinos, auditorium, museum, aquarium and over two dozen restaurants. The Pierce Hotel in Tampa was a world favorite mainly because of its famous artificial beach. With global harsh climates barely reaching above sixty-five degrees in the summer, and most of the beaches still showing scars from the last world war, it was refreshing childhood memory for most of the rich and famous to visit a sandy beach equipped with a large body of salt water and its own eco-system.

The corporate office was a sixty-eight story skyscraper famous for its unique twisting architecture, elaborate exits, tunnels, and clear glass hallways. At night, red and white LED lights illuminated the building's exterior and highlighted the Pierce family insignia on the corner of the widest face of the building. While the hotel showcased a white marble and stone exterior, the corporate office's exterior was made up with dense bulletproof glass that was able to change color according to a button that an operator would choose weekly. It usually stayed a light color that matched its neighboring hotel, but it would often show a clear mirror that would come out on cloudy days.

When it came to the strict security the hotel possessed, the corporate office was in a class of its own. Each floor was patrolled by thirty armed Black Creek soldiers incognito. All employees, including both upper and middle management had to wear a visible ID tag over their left breast pocket at all times or they would be susceptible to detainment. The main access to every floor had palm and retina scanners. Every elevator had electronic sensors that detected stress and body heat. An alarm would sound if anything was out of the ordinary, that along with automatic sentry guns that would pop out of the wall panels.

While the hotel chain was the Pierce Corporation's main source of income, it was also the parent company of dozens of other lucrative businesses. Isaac Pierce was a shareholder of Garrett and Moss Financial, a billion dollar investment firm who's dished out loans to nearly every big business in the American Empire. The frivolous young Benjamin Garrett pretty much inherited the CEO position of Garrett and Moss. But Benjamin wasn't half the accountant his father was. With businesses declaring bankruptcy and owners forfeiting on their loans, Benjamin didn't hesitate when Isaac's eldest son, the now deceased Albert, approached with the idea of a partnership.

Black Creek Securities was financed by Garrett and Moss financial. Jonathan Lamb, the pious original founder of the firm, fell prey to a web of lies and deception after he declined the olive branch of a partnership from a man named Michael Helms. Helms ended up paying off Black Creek soldiers to assassinate a South Carolinian candidate for Governor and then presented evidence of Black Creek's involvement to have Jonathan Lamb arrested and executed for treason. Helms took over as the President and owner of Black Creek, pledging to restore the company as the Empire's "ace in the hole" premier private military firm. Michael Helms was a childhood friend of Isaac's late son, Charlie.

The last major acquisition for the Pierce Corporation was their sister company Tsukishima Industries based in the Shinjuku district of Tokyo, Japan. Tsukishima Industries was the world's leading pioneer of cybernetic engineering, cognitive prosthetic synthesizing and biogenetics. Tsukishima racked in billions for their production of androids and the many critical prosthetic implants used on individuals scarred and disfigured from the wars. It was more universally utilized when it came to maiming incidents involving the world's propensity for settling things with swords since the prices of bullets and gunpowder skyrocketed.

Thanks to Tsukishima's research, surgeons now had the ability to link their patients mind to their new implants, allowing them to mentally control their cybernetic or prosthetic limbs as if they were born with it.

Tsukishima Industries has a dark side to their heroic endeavors, however. Through their biogenetic research, the company was able to produce the Furyx Gene. Nearly a thousand test subjects died over the course of two decades before the Gene Modification Department saw its first success.

Due to an extensive investigation that nearly ruined the company, Takeshi Tsukishima enlisted the help of Japan's most influential yakuza oyabun (godfather), Die Amaruto. Amaruto, in turn, asked for the help of Isaac Pierce. Isaac got his associate Bosco Rosenberg to offer up an American drug dealer, who he was going to kill anyway, as a fall guy to Japanese officials. The media outlets painted Tsukishima Industries out to be the victim and the American was executed as a mass-murdering terrorist. Die Amaruto was granted a large share of the company and Isaac Pierce was made a partner in the company. Thus the binding chains between the Pierce and the Japan's largest yakuza group were welded.

On the rooftop of Pierce's corporate office, a transport helicopter was descending on the helipad. The luxury helicopter was painted sleek black with the red Pierce family insignia donned on the tinted windows. The propellers kicked up dust that glittered in the bright flood lights. For security purposes, there wasn't a single shaded area on the rooftop. Snipers lined every corner. Sixteen Black Creek soldiers wearing fancy cloaks that hid long thin spears lined up double file in rows of eight, waiting in militaristic fashion for the chopper's doors to open.

A latch on the helicopter turned. The door electronically protruded out and slid open. Then out stepped the man, Isaac Pierce. He was accompanied by his longtime friend, business partner and CFO Melissa Krauss. Both were dressed warmly in comfortable electronically heated overcoats. Both were wearing computerized sunglasses that automatically adjusted to either block out the glare of the flood lights, or brighten the shades of darkness. The Black Creek soldiers all greeted in unison with a bow a sign of respect Isaac adapted from his Japanese friend, Die Amaruto. Without saying a word, Isaac led Ms. Krauss and four attorneys toward the building's glass sliding access doors.

At sixty-five, Isaac was still healthy and outgoing. He had a baldhead with distinguished wrinkles above his eyebrows. He should've been walking with a cane, but managed without it because he thought it cliché for someone of his stature. Ms. Krauss was about a decade younger, but more aggressive and prim. She was a stout figure with brown hair and cold blue eyes donned with glasses of thin golden frames. Blessed with eidetic memory, Ms. Krauss didn't keep an electric organizer with dates and numbers since she had it all in her head. The only reason why she needed her twelve assistants was because Isaac found it more convenient to give her the order by which she'd pass on and delegate.

It was close to 2am and the two were just now returning from a dinner with Mayor Bayne and Bishop Battalgia. Bishop Battalgia was both an influential Catholic Bishop and a bulldog of a Florida State senator, using religious and patriotic guilt to stay in power. Battalgia was a well-known opponent of Isaac's rising power and has issued threats of Imperial sanctioned inspections of many Pierce Corp. facilities. While Battalgia was too important to kill, Isaac was able to convince the senator to remain silent through indirect threats of data manipulation. On top of that, Isaac had proof and witnesses who could testify that Battalgia's campaign advisors had illegally hacked into his campaign accounts and siphoned funds into his own.

In a private underground garage of the corporate building, the three SUVs from earlier were just now filing in after passing through a checkpoint. They came to a slow park at a designated space right in front of an elevator lobby. A group of high-end female impersonating androids, all dressed professionally in skirt uniforms, stood waiting to tend to the wounded and scan the vehicles of any blood, bullets and incriminating evidence.

Lazar watched as two female soldiers slowly carried out their dead male counterparts from one of the SUVs. "You ladies did a good job, eh. We shall all pray for our fallen comrades." He whispered aloud. The soldiers nodded, grateful for his sentiments.

Sean, Braden, Adam and Forest had given the android attendants their coats, accessories and weapons and were already standing on the opened elevator. Only Braden still had his katana by his side. From his training, he learned how to dismantle and clean the blade himself and no way was he going to trust any manmade machine with the job. So they stood waiting for Lazar, slightly annoyed that he took the time to complement the other soldiers before they were taken off to the in-house infirmary. Lazar picked up on their attitudes and shook his head as he walk onto the elevator.

"The least you cold bastards could do is encourage them." Lazar admonished.

Adam pressed a button for the 32nd floor before entering his thumbprint into a scanner. Sean and Forest weren't cold, as Lazar put it, but were more so just exhausted and tired. They couldn't wait to check into their personal hotel suites.

Just as the brightly lit elevator started to ascend, Braden brushed past Adam to press the button for the 28th floor. Adam gave him a puzzled look. "What are you doing? You know we have to debrief." Adam asked him.

"I will. I need to check something first." Braden told him.

Adam sighed as he reached into his pocket and took out his glasses to put on. "Whatever."

After passing the third floor, the glass elevator walls showed the scenic view of the city and the magnificence of the massive glowing Halo. While Sean and Forest took such views for granted, Braden always stood in awe of it. He loved heights and had a greater love for breathtaking views. When going out on long trips by car or plane, most need some kind of game or movie playing to keep them entertained. Braden didn't need such things. He was always satisfied with simply looking out the window at the water, the snow, the trees or the architecture of the bridges while passing over the bay. His own mind was all the entertainment he needed. And such views sparked his imagination.

There was a soft chime as the elevator gradually slowed down. Braden exited onto the 28th floor as planned. He could feel Adam's skeptical gaze following him. "We'll be waiting." Adam reminded. Braden ignored the quip and continued on.

The 28th floor of the building was the central nervous system for surveillance over the entire Pierce Empire. The feed from every camera of every entity, business, or property owned by the Pierce came through to the 28th floor. Hundreds of prosthetic androids codenamed Nymphs were used in place of potentially guilty-conscious employees to spot any activity that seemed nefarious or out of the ordinary. The nymphs, all named by assigned numbers, had the seductively realistic appearance of a young woman, all with the same figure and bust, but were differentiated by a variety of hairstyles or make up. They all wore the same black business skirts and tight buttoned up white collared shirts. Each nymph was equipped with a special program of artificial intelligence that made it easy for the four human floor managers to communicate and confirm or invalidate their suspicions.

The main bullpen of the 28th floor was a massive half-moon shaped auditorium that descended at an incline row by row down to the bottom. To make it easy on the nymph's optical sensors, there were no overhead lights but only soft shaded blue floodlights along the walls near the floor. The nymphs all sat in front of their own station that consisted of two monitors and the latest upgraded computer operating systems. Their stations faced a huge wall that showed six large wall mounted screens. Each screen showed a different feed that was put up by the floor managers whenever there was busy activity in a specific area.

Other than the bathrooms and main control room where the floor managers operated a half a million-dollar control board, there was another room on the floor that was unofficially referred to as the Hackers Hub. It was the only room on the floor that required a both a keypad password, a thumbprint as well a second-remote party to give access. The door was both bullet and blast proof. And even if an intruder managed to bust the door down, there were escape routes in place for the employees inside.

In the Hackers Hub, over thirty of the world's most gifted computer whiz-kids were hired to hack e-mail addresses, IP addresses, satellite access, bank accounts, wireless hard drives and of course any surveillance feed connected to the net. When a gang was ordered to complete a mission under direct orders of Isaac Pierce, it was up to the hackers to hack into any camera feed that may be recording the act and either alter it, blur out faces, or destroy it altogether.

That being said, the moment Braden stepped foot in the room, all of the typing and small chatter came to an abrupt stop. The hackers were stunned. They were all mostly young college grad students or middle-aged otakus. All of them signed over some kind of collateral that could be used to haunt them should they divulge any secrets. Other than the company's board of directors, most of the employees who worked for both Pierce Corporation and even Black Creek were oblivious to who Braden was. Most had only heard of his name and chalked the rumors up to an exaggeration spread by those who were easily impressed. But in that dark computer lab, everyone knew what Braden looked like. They knew what he was capable of. Needless to say, they were terrified out of their fucking minds.

The dimly lit room had three rows of eight stations. Each station was equipped with a computer and three 24-inch monitor screens. With sixteen headphone wearing hackers on the floor at the moment, Braden helped himself to sit at an empty station, propping the handle of his sword against the desk. Then, he moved the mouse to get out of the screen saver and typed in his username and password to bring up his own personal settings.

The closest hackers to him were Mariah and her boyfriend Derek, two grad students working to pay their way through film school. Mariah was petite and blond with glasses, while Derek was of German descent, short and in serious need of cardio training. Braden was still wearing the dark scraped up turtleneck from earlier. He smelled of smoke and his upper back was exposed.

Mariah and Derek looked at each other, both sensing the same nervous tension. Mariah, the more adventurous of the two and closer to Braden, cautiously wheeled her chair over two stations and leaned over. Surprisingly, Braden didn't appear to have noticed her. In her quick peak, she was able to see Braden opening up video files from a folder and quickly closing them before opening up another video file.

Then, she hastily scooted herself back to her own station with her mouth wide open in a smirk of infatuation. Derek raised his hand and beckoned for some kind of explanation from her. It was dead silent save from the hum of the computer fans. All of the other hackers were wide-eyed under high arching eyebrows. They too awaited Mariah's response. Finally, she managed to mouth the words in a childish whisper, "He's hot." Almost every guy rolled their eyes before returning them to their monitors. The curiosity in the women, however, was amplified, each of them struggling to catch a glance.

Satisfied, Mariah got back to work at her computer station. An instant message chatbox appeared on her screen. "What's he doing here?" Derek asked via text.

Mariah grinned as she typed back. "I dunno. I think he's looking for something. Should I see if he needs help?"

Almost as soon as she sent the message, Derek replied back. "NO!! You know what he can do? Firing us is the least of my concerns. And his sword is right freaking there! Seriously, Mariah. Just wait till he freaking LEAVES!"

Mariah found Derek's concerns to be very endearing. She listened. She could hear Braden still clicking on the mouse frantically. Her heart started to pound. She clicked back into the surveillance footage she was assigned to, but an impulse was yanking at her. She bit the nail of her thumb and leaned over her keyboard, wondering what to do. She considered Derek's warning. She knew he was right. Mariah had only been a hacker for three months and had already witnessed Braden end over half a dozen lives. She was sitting next to a serial killer and yet, Braden seemed like a rock star to her. Just as she wiped the sweat from her forehead and pulled the bangs from her vision, she heard the sounds of small plastic rolling on the granite flooring.

"Excuse me..." Mariah jumped at the sound of Braden's voice. Embarrassed, she covered her mouth and tried to regain control of her breathing. Braden wasn't surprised by her behavior. He wasn't annoyed or flattered. He just wanted her assistance.

"Yes?" Mariah squeaked.

"Can you help me with something?" Braden asked politely.

"Oh. Yes! Of course!" Mariah exclaimed. Everyone gawked with horror as they watched Mariah rise from her chair to follow Braden back to his station.

She pulled on the bottom of her wrinkled shirt to straighten it out as she stood over Braden. "Um…If you're looking for the footage from tonight, we already scrubbed your faces from the film." She told him.

"You were really cool, by the way!" Derek shouted in a loud flamboyant pitch out of nowhere, inciting several quick noted snickers and gasps.

"Sorry about him. We all saw you tonight. You were amazing." Mariah blabbered out from embarrassment.

"Thank you. Can you pull up the footage anyway?" Braden asked her.

"Oh sure! Um. Let's see here." Mariah said as she leaned over him and typed on his keyboard.

Braden noticed Mariah's fingers shaking as she typed. He then looked up to truly examine her. The controlled muscles in her face were trying their best to contain her smile. Her eyes seemed strained and focused on one spot of the screen. It was then that Braden was suddenly flattered and found her self-control both adorable and admirable.

"Here you go. It's much quicker to just use the search function. I mean, I can show you how to navigate the Calliance system. But I don't think you'd want to sit here through all that." Mariah told him before standing upright, prim and proper.

Braden said nothing, but smiled at her with empathy. Mariah held back her smile, but couldn't hold back her blushing. "Whelp! All of the video files from the airport are in that folder. If you need anything else, just let me know. I'm um…right over here." Mariah concluded with a nervous giggle.

Braden smirked before turning to the computer monitor. "Thank you, Mariah. You've been really helpful." He said. Mariah accidentally bowed to him. Then she wondered why she bowed to him before returning to her chair.

Braden clicked on a specific video feed, not of the fight, but of the airport. After pressing play, he scrubbed through the footage, fast forwarding with five second increments. Suddenly, the thick plated door to the room opened. All of the hackers all turned to see another unexpected guess. Braden didn't need to turn. From the sounds of clicking heels, expensive jewelry and bold scent of spiced perfume; he could tell it was none other than his older cousin, Cassandra.

Cassie leaned against the door with one hand on those perfectly curved hips. She watched the back of Braden and smirked that he didn't look her way as she was accustomed to most men doing. The hackers watched and listened as Cassie stepped forward, one stiletto boot at a time.

At 27, Cassie was the top Black Creek agent in the TIU. The Tactical Intelligence Unit was made up of specialist trained in disguise, escape, concealment, poisons and a multitude of covert skills used for more clandestine missions. On occasion, the TIU was assigned the assassinations that needed to be executed by more discreet means.

Unlike other agents, Cassie usually wore an expensive designer's outfit that consisted of long black skirt and a classy white top that accentuated her sculpted double-Ds. Her long black hair was always well fashioned in some $500 style. While her father was Isaac Pierce's younger brother, of African descent, her mother was a former blond blue-eyed supermodel. Inheriting her mother's good looks and light skin tone, Cassie was also tall, almost standing a full six feet.

Cassie was one of the few people on earth who Braden actually cherished. And other than Lazar, Cassie was the only other person he confided in. Ever since Braden was little, Cassie always knew he was different. But Cassie liked different. Growing up, Cassie always had her pick of any guy she wanted. But she learned early on how most guys were the same. The same whims. The same desires. But Braden was different. To Cassie, there was an unlimited feeling of depth to him. So much that she herself couldn't understand or comprehend.

Cassie favored Braden so much that she named him godfather to her own four-year-old son, Alexander. Alex was conceived during Cassie's mission where she was to seduce an Arabian prince. She killed the prince and kept the son.

"Brady, what are you doing in here?" Cassandra asked in a naturally husky, seductive voice that could get the blood of any man flowing. She walked over and put her arms around Braden's shoulders before running her fingertips across the back of his damaged turtleneck.

"Oh my god, Braden. Are you alright? What happened?" Cassie asked.

"Fell off a plane." Braden answered.

"The plane that blew up? It's all over the news? You know David's not going to be too happy about this." Cassie said as she reached and rolled over a chair. As she sat down next to him, she noticed the other hackers watching her. She quickly raised her left hand and gave a sharp echoing snap. Everyone hurried to get back to work.

"I swear, why is everyone so worried about him? Who cares if he's upset or not? People act like his anger moves mountains." Braden replied as he continued to scrub the film.

"Well, maybe not mountains. Hmm…I suppose I know what you mean. But ever since he was named treasurer, he's been strutting around here like he's hot stuff." Cassie said, crossing her legs and propping her head up with an elbow on the desk.

"So what if he does? How does that affect you in any way, shape or form?" Braden asked.

"That's not the point. You know I can't stand it when people think they're my superior."

"Bit hypocritical coming from you, is it not? Miss high and mighty who doesn't like to touch door handles." Braden pointed out with a smirk.

"Yes, well. People don't like to wash their hands, do they? And I'm no hypocrite. Shame on you, Braden. I never said it was wrong to think yourself superior. I just don't like it when it's done to me. To hell with the golden rule." Cassie said with a haughty smile of her own.

After a long pause in conversation with Cassie silently watching him in admiration, Braden finally popped out a question that's been on his mind for a while. Turning to her, Braden asked with a sincere expression, "Cassandra. When are you going to take the Furyx Gene?"

Cassie furrowed her eyebrows. It was a subject she had already made clear to others. "Braden... I'm still upset with you for taking it."

"Why? I don't understand. What's the big deal?" Braden demanded to know.

Cassie scoffed. "You could've died, you imbecile. I still have nightmares of you shaking when you took it. Do you know how painful it was for me to see you like that? To hear you screaming at the top of your lungs! I thought you were going to die. Not to mention it's only fueled your ego." Cassie said, gradually raising her voice.

"What ego?" Braden whispered back.

She wheeled closer to him and gave him a stern look. "Like tonight! You're way too reckless! Did you think Furyx would protect your falling off that plane in midflight? What's next? A plunge off the Skyway Bridge?"

Braden glared at her. He spoke aggressively, yet softly so that only she would hear. "If you already knew that I fell off a jet in midflight, then why on earth did you ask what happened to me? Its talk like that which makes me hard to trust those of your circle. No one's straightforward. You prevaricate and toss around your rhetorical artifices hoping I'll slip up and say something revealing. As if you don't already know."

Cassie was taken aback by his attitude, but stood her ground. "Braden, I'm serious. You need to take better care of yourself. You may think it's just you out there, but I've been cleaning up after you since you were nine. You're like a little brother to me. You should consider this when pulling out all the stops for something as insignificant as eliminating an enemy that can be killed at a later time."

Braden understood her concern and took it in. After slightly shaking his head, he turned back to his monitors and continued scrubbing the footage. "You're right. I won't bring it up again."

Cassie watched him. Her sullen look of anger quickly faded back to fascination. "You're just worried about me. Aren't you?" Cassie said as she pinched his shoulder.

"Damn!" Braden whispered as shot up from his seat.

"What's wrong?" Cassie said with a puzzled amusement.

"Cass. I'm not going crazy, but for the past few weeks there's been a stranger who's been following me. He was at the airport tonight. But this stupid security set up has too many freaking blind spots." Braden complained while maintaining his calm composure.

Cassie took the opportunity to taunt. "That's not like you. To let witnesses get away."

Braden headed for the door. "This isn't funny, Cassie. It's freaking irritating. The next time I see this bastard, I'm having his throat slit."

"How do you know it's not a girl? A secret admirer!" Cassie teased. Braden simply waved goodbye to her before leaving the room.

Up on the 32nd floor, Sean, Forrest, and Lazar had already been debriefed and were on their way back down the elevators to head for the hotel. Adam waited alone in Isaac's executive condo sized office. Even though David had his own office, he spent most of his time in his father's room, always wanting to stay on top of things. That's why Adam chose to wait for David there.

The office had high vaulted ceilings and was lit by golden lamp fixtures attached to the walls, gifts given to Isaac from a former Russian Prime Minister. Modern Japanese imported black leather couches, dark brown polished coffee tables and stands that held statues and lamps furnished the office on cappuccino colored stone flooring.

Laid back and at ease, Adam was gazing out the theater sized windows toward the hotel, specifically the fire that oozed from a small-scale model of a volcano in the front lot. When David entered, Adam's back was turned toward the door. David was accompanied by three attorneys, but he gestured for them to wait outside before he closed the door.

David was in his late-thirties, tall, dark, and handsome. He kept in good shape and looks sharp with his finely trimmed mustache and goatee. Enjoying the fruits of labor, he spared no expense in dressing in the finest designer's suits. He always carried some brand of cigar inside his breast pocket along with concealed handgun in a vest holster.

David Pierce was the fourth eldest of old man Isaac's five sons and the only one still alive. Over the course of two decades, Isaac's sons were extremely instrumental in shaping the Pierce Empire to what it is today and they paid for it with their own blood. In some cases, with the blood of their wives and children. It wasn't easy for Isaac to lose his sons to the likes of the Five Pillars and other rival factions, but no one took it more personal than their only surviving brother. David swore to himself that he'd never let their deaths go in vain…even if it took making decisions that gave him the reputation of Pierce Corp.'s very own demon.

"Adam. How could you let this happen?" David asked, managing to hold back his frustrations well.

Adam smirked, keeping his gaze on the volcano. For some reason, he predicted those would be the first words out of David's mouth.

Adam turned around and prepared to make his defense. "Sir. I told them…"

"I sent you out there…You! You Adam! I sent you out there specifically to contain my baby cousins and not let Braden have his way." David said in a stern, yet surprisingly reasonable tone.

Adam shook his head and nodded. "You're right sir. No excuses."

With a heavy sigh, David put his hands in his pocket and approached. "You and I came up together, Adam. You, Michael and myself. Now look at Mike. Practically running Black Creek like it's his own. I want to see you stay with us for a long time. But I need to know you're capable. Reliable. This shit right here. It's not a convincing performance, my man."

David's words penetrated Adam to the core. His disappointed gaze did more work than any boxer could do on Adam's pride as a man. Just then, there was an electronic chime. David and Adam turned toward to door to see Isaac and Ms. Krauss coming in. The elder Pierce could sense the tension in the room and after a day of his own strenuous debates, Isaac found it all very amusing. He sighed with a smile as he took off his overcoat and neatly placed it on a golden coat hanger. Ms. Krauss closed the door and followed Isaac toward his desk.

"I'll call Mr. Ruth in the morning. He's had enough time to review our proposal." Ms. Krauss said as she planted some affidavits on the desk in front of him. "I'm calling it a night, Isaac. You should too."

"Yes. Yes." Isaac nodded as he situated himself in front of the polished oak wood desk. He pressed one of several metal buttons implanted in the desk in front of the phone. Two 54-inch panels in the wall protruded out and separated, revealing two flat LED screens. David and Adam both just stood in the center of the room watching Isaac and Ms. Krauss like students awaiting their lessons.

Ms. Krauss chuckled. "You two look like you've just brought a horse into a china shop. Something you don't want us to see on the telly?"

"What's wrong with you, boys?" Isaac had to ask.

David shook his head as he approached. He reached for the remote and turned on one of the TVs. It was already set on a 24 hour bay news channel. "Braden's getting out of control, Papa. The boy took down a private jet in midflight, leaving behind a signature for all to see his handy work. This is bad publicity. Everyone and their mothers knows it was him."

Adam walked over to the mini bar and casually poured himself a drink. Ms. Krauss approached him with a malicious grin. "And where were you?" Ms. Krauss asked.

Adam turned around to see she was talking to him. Adam squinted his eyes and thought carefully of what next to say. Even though Adam and Ms. Krauss have been stepping on each other's shoes since David brought him on board, Ms. Krauss has in a sense, acted as Adam's special mentor. She fully believed that one day Adam would take her place as an unofficial consigliore.

"I thought Braden's actions would send out an example to our opposition. If Braden's willing to go to such lengths as to take out a goddamn airplane, who knows what he'd do if he really gave a damn."

Adam took a sip of whiskey, confident in his answer. Ms. Kraus smiled, impressed with not just his answer but with his attitude to her challenge.

"Don't worry about your cousin, David. Braden is simple-minded. He sees one objective and does whatever it takes to accomplish it. That's exactly why he's priceless. Anything else is unintentional."

Isaac spoke while he was diligently looking over the affidavits, signing on the dotted lines. David nodded before he walked over to sit in one of two leather chairs in front of Isaac's desk. Adam soon joined him, leaving Ms. Krauss to linger behind Adam's chair to see what else would be discussed.

"Even so. He should lay low for a while. This incident with the airport…Mylanta is already putting together a team of publicists to combat this. But the rumors will spread from the police to the journalists, to Rosenberg's crew, to the other Ybor families. They'll have their eyes peeled for anyone who remotely resembles him." David said.

Isaac lowered his eyebrows at the thought. "We went through great lengths to train Braden well."

"Going so far as to hire Takizawa from Renji." Ms. Krauss added.

"More like hide Takizawa for Renji in which he just so happens to have trained Braden in the meantime." David chimed in.

"Do you mean Guile Takizawa? I thought he was an exclusive Japanese nationalist. Heard he only trained the sons of high ranking yakuzas. Not us gaijins." Adam asked.

Ms. Krauss smiled as she rubbed Adam's shoulders. "You mean you don't know? Braden's mentoring was a gift from the Kusanagi-Gumi. In a soft persuasion to limit our expansion in land of the rising sun."

"The point is..." Isaac said, rolling his eyes at Ms. Krauss with a charming smile. "Braden knows his limits. In the five years he's been in the field, not a single frame of his face has surfaced and he's always finished the job. All the money in that casino can't buy that level of dependency."

David nodded with a sullen expression before taking a sip from a glass Adam handed him. Sensing the conversation was over, Ms. Krauss turned to take her leave and exit the room. Adam noted David's lack of satisfaction and found the opportunity to make up for his previous failure.

"Perhaps…It would be a good idea for Braden, Sean and Forrest to take a brief vacation from their active status. It'll be good for all of them. A reward for their work in Chile and a kind gesture from you."

David grinned as he added. "That's right, Papa. When's the last time you bought them anything?"

Isaac looked at the two of them and smiled. Turning a page to the next document, Isaac continued signing papers and uttered, "Perhaps…"

David and Adam brought their glasses in to a tap with a soft chime. Leaving Isaac to chuckle to himself, saying, "Boys will be boys."

Chapter 9: Enter Eliza Christie

After finishing up at the Clearwater airstrip, Inspector Gazi spent the whole night in his office at the precinct downtown. With only plain black coffee in his system, he painstakingly scrubbed through surveillance footage. It didn't take him long to realize the footage had been tampered with. But who was he going to complain to? The footage looked flawless other than the fact that the face of every Black Creek agent had been blurred out by frame interlacing. After putting fourteen hours on the job, Gazi decided to call it a day at 11am.

The clouds that moved in through the night had moved on by morning. Clear sunny skies and a brisk icy wind had taken over. Gazi drove through his neighborhood longing for a hot shower and at least six hours of sleep. His townhouse was in the Green Trees subdivision not far from downtown Tampa. It was an upscale gated community with security guards and cameras on every lamppost. A large beautiful pond and the landscaped trees that surrounded it provided an ideal community for citizens to come out for a nice jog or watch the sunset over the horizon.

The gold luxury sedan pulled in over a dull red cobblestone driveway. Gazi took off his sunglasses as he opened the door. There was strain in his back muscles as he fought to crawl out of his car. Ignoring the half-empty cup of tea in his cup holder, he pulled out his briefcase from the passenger seat and closed the car door. On his way to his front door, he noticed that the small maple tree in his neighbor's yard was beginning to lose its leaves already.

"It's still August for Christ's sake." He mumbled to himself.

Upon entering the front door, Gazi was greeted by none other than his beloved Rottweiler. His house was spotlessly clean. He had a knack for interior design and all things modern. His living room held a black, grey and white theme to it with black wood lacquer flooring, stylish grey carpets and curtains complete with a white couch set.

In the foyer, Gazi stood with his back toward a large glass trophy cabinet. Next to the cabinet was a series of fashionably placed hooks attached to the wall. Gazi hung his keys and coat up on the hooks while examining his numerous accolades and photos of his former partner. He did this routine everyday upon entering and exiting the house, constantly reminding himself why he fought so hard in a system where corruption seemingly had no bounds.

"Hey Max." Gazi said with a gentle smile as he finally got around to petting the dog. "Long day. How was yours? Stayed out of my closet, I hope."

Gazi sighed with relief before heading for the living room, loosening up his tie and turning up the heat on his AC unit. Suddenly, something caught his attention. It was movement he detected in the reflection of the AC unit's tiny LED panel. Whipping his head around, Gazi peered into his dining room and there she was, sitting at the table looking over a stack of college brochures and paper work for financial aid. Aware that she was being watched, Eliza smiled before lifting her green-eyed gaze from the brochures to an exhausted Gazi.

The sight of her slowly ascending out of her chair to stand took Gazi's breath away. At the age of 19, Eliza was almost as tall as he was. Her curly hair was now longer and straighter, fashioned into a more professional look. Her skin wasn't as tan as before, but still a healthy even glow. She was still wearing her favorite light-green hooded overcoat over a buttoned up white blouse and blue jeans. She was gorgeous.

Gazi couldn't stop himself from smiling as Eliza approached with a beaming smile of her own. The two embraced each other in a warm hug. Eliza started laughing, finding his astonishment all too amusing.

"Oh my god. Look at you!" Gazi whimpered, completely breaking character from the hardball detective he's known to be.

Eliza finally managed to contain her laughter as she tucked some hair behind her right ear. "It's good to see you, Gazi. I missed you."

"I missed YOU!" Gazi exclaimed. "What did…Why didn't you tell me you were coming back? I would've straightened up. Made you a room."

Eliza laughed. "It was kind of a spur of the moment thing. School's right around the corner and I…I just know I wanted to finished my education here. Where my home is." Eliza explained.

"Oh my gosh." Gazi said. "Well, we got to go out and celebrate. Are you hungry? Have you eaten yet? Let's go get something to eat. I know a place. Come on, you'll love it." Gazi said with excitement as he backtracked toward the door.

Eliza wasn't hungry and had other plans, but knew it was rare for Gazi to be so upbeat. She turned back toward the dining room. There was a green duffel bag amongst her black suitcases. She wondered if it would be safe to leave it there in the open. After hearing Gazi's beckoning call, Eliza abandoned her concern and hurried to catch up.

It seemed just like yesterday that Eliza was in the passenger seat of Gazi's golden sedan. Gazi was heading northwest on Memorial Highway toward the Town and Country district. They had just past underneath the Halo and Eliza could see the bay in the distance. The nostalgia was bone chilling. It had only been four years, but she could tell Tampa's development had increase significantly. The streets seemed cleaner with new pavement and painted signals. There were more trees and bushes planted along the mediums and shoulders. For a moment, it was hard to tell Tampa was still the same Tampa she knew.

"Eliza?" Gazi called out.

Eliza turned with a smile. "Hmm?"

"Did you just hear me?" He asked.

"Oh. I'm sorry, Gazi. I was just thinking. It's been so long. The bay. The sky. The Halo. It's all…Tampa Bay is incredible." Eliza gushed.

Gazi nodded. "Not much has changed. Things are still…"

"Shouldn't you be asleep?" Eliza interrupted. "It's really not a big deal to get breakfast it's almost lunch time anyway. You must be tired from working all night. Especially after last night."

Gazi pondered for a moment, wondering what she knew, or even if it was a good idea to divulge how his night really went. "You saw the news?" He asked.

Eliza nodded. "Crazy stuff, yeah? You never told me you were promoted to Inspector though. Does Boa know? I know she'd be proud of you."

Gazi smiled and sighed. "I sure do miss that girl."

"You should go visit her sometime. And you should see your niece and nephew now. Cloud and Rain. They're a hoot. Cloud's just now starting high school. I kind of feel bad that I won't be there to ask him about his first day. But I talked to him about girls so he should be alright." Eliza said with a chuckle.

The thought of his baby sister and her children made Gazi's heart heavy. Eliza noticed the water well in his eyes as he struggled to focus on the road. Then, she noticed the scar below his left eye, but didn't want to ask about it.

"Here it is." Gazi said before coming to a slow halt in a parallel parking spot.

The Rustic Street Plaza was a market square, lined with an assortment of different vendors and restaurants. Eliza stepped out to see that they were parked in front of diner that featured a classy botanical theme to it. Tables were set up outside in the front patio of the diner. The patio enclosed by designed twisting black rail fences with small elegant white angel figurines dwindling from the edge. Green vines were intertwined throughout the high metal railing arch that made up its entrance.

"Magnificent isn't it." Gazi said as he walked around the car to take Eliza by the arm.

"Yes. It looks beautiful." Eliza marveled.

"Yeah, well. I remembered your obsession with light-green." Gazi pointed out.

Eliza playfully gasped. "It's not an obsession you ass."

"Oh! There's the Eliza I know." Gazi said in laughter.

"The color is Peridot." Eliza clarified.

Gazi escorted her to an outdoor table near a marble bust of an ancient Roman emperor. It was near a manageable 68 degrees outside but well worth the view of the clear blue skies and vibrant horticulture. A waitress approached with a palm-size electronic tablet in hand. Gazi ordered a decaffeinated cappuccino with extra crème while Eliza ordered a bacon and ricotta omelet with water. As she ordered, Gazi couldn't take his eyes off of her. It was hard to get over her astounding metamorphosis. It was like that dark shadow that had been following her had been lifted. With her cheerful smile and bright green eyes, to Gazi, Eliza seemed like a brand new day.

"So are you going to miss Korea? Boa told me how much you two enjoyed those capoeira lessons together. She said you were a natural. And you even took up painting! You'll have to paint something for me. To liven up our living room." Gazi said.

Eliza nodded as she pondered. "The last four years feels like… a cocoon. That's not to say that I um…felt fettered or restrained, but it was more so a period that I used to really grow from the little brat I used to be. And now that I'm back in Tampa, I'm ready to spread my wings like a butterfly and reach for the sky." Eliza said with inspirational confidence in exuding in each syllable.

The proud yet goofy looking smile stretching across Gazi's face made Eliza burst out in laughter. "Oh my god, Gazi! What?"

"I don't know. I… Looking at you now kind of forces me to put things into perspective. In a sense, I'm envious of your sanguine outlook. So young. At the start of your journey with so much road in front of you. I'm proud of you, Elizabeth."

Eliza reached over and grabbed his hand in earnest. "You're not alone, Angel. I'm here now. And I promise I'll never leave this place again. We're family, you and I."

The waitress returned with their drinks and a basket of buttery poppy seed rolls. Eliza let go of Gazi's hand and sat back in her chair. "Thank you." Eliza told the waitress who politely nodded and walked off.

"So, tell me about Mr. Hideo Shikagane." Gazi said, mispronouncing every syllable of the name. "I've only met him once or twice but he didn't exactly seem like Mr. Personality. Boa loves him, so I'll continuing giving him the benefit of a doubt."

Eliza took a drink of water before putting the glass back on the table. The shimmer of the bracelet she was wearing slightly distracted her from answering. "Mr. Hide wasn't that bad. I may have run into him once or twice. But I mostly hung out with Rain and Cloud. The little ankle biters."

Gazi smiled. "And how is my nephew doing? Is he an athlete? For the love of god, tell me we have athlete in the family." Gazi said while breaking a roll in half.

Eliza nodded. "He is pretty gifted as an athlete. He's short though. I'm taller than him."

"We'll you're almost taller than me, girl!" Gazi said with laughter. "Did you play any sports or participate in extracurricular activities?"

"Um. I did a little bit of everything, Gazi. But mostly got into philosophy and competed in debates."

"Really?" Gazi said with intrigue.

"Yes. Philosophy was one of the first tools I used to climb out of the hole I was in. Live this life as though you've one life to live and live it with a clear conscience. If your conscience is clouding your goal of happiness, then identify what's standing in your way and detach yourself from it." She recited.

Gazi squinted his eyes, racing to recall where he heard such talk. Then it hit him. "Ah. Reginald Harvey, eh? August the 18th."

Eliza giggled. "Gazi, you have no idea how much that book changed my life."

"Well you know Harvey was a rebel to traditions amongst other things. Is that what you are? Still a rebel?" Gazi asked, jokingly pounding his fist on the table with a stern glare.

Eliza nodded with a serious look of sarcasm. "Oh yes. And a hardcore rebel at that."

Gazi smiled. "So! You'll be applying for the Medici then?"

"No need. I received my acceptance letter last month. Would've been foolish to turn it down, I think." Eliza said with a haughty smile, tilting her head ever so slightly to brag.

"That's good news. Getting into the Medici is no easy feat. Most of the lieutenants on the force failed their entrance exam many times before finally getting in. What's your major?"

"Criminology. But to minor in art, of course. Can't go dull on my brushstrokes." Eliza told him.

"Good. Good. I'll have my guest room set up for you." Gazi offered.

Eliza gave an uneasy grin of uncertainty. "Gazi... As much as you know I love you. I won't want to stay with you for too long. Eventually, I'll want to get my own apartment."

"With what money? Are you going to get a job? I know you'll want your independence but in this economy, it's much better if you stay with me." Gazi told her.

"No. You'll feel much better if I stay with you." Eliza pointed out. "And I'm not hard pressed for cash. I still have seventy-five grand; from my father's insurance policy remember."

"Oh…" Gazi uttered, slightly recoiling in his hope.

"But I'll probably want to come over on the weekends and like, every other night. You know. Free food and all." Eliza laughed.

"Is that what you're going to put in your phone? When your phone rings from me, the name will come up 'free food'? You got another thing coming." Gazi laughed.

The waitress returned with Eliza's entrée. She clapped her hands with joy before reaching for a knife and fork. Gazi laughed at the adorable childish mannerism that he knew she was just exaggerating. Reaching for his coffee mug, Gazi finally let out the first thing that's been on his mind since seeing Eliza.

"It's good to have you back, Eliza." With her mouth full, Eliza simply looked up to him, nodded, and raised a thumb up.

Within the hour, Eliza let Gazi get some much needed rest while she went off for registration day. Tampa was home to the largest, most financially endowed institution of higher learning in the world. Since the year 2150, the Tampa Metropolitan University, affectionately known as the Medici, has produced some of the world's foremost thinkers, political leaders and liberal artists. Of the two million students that applied every year from around the world, only the top eight thousand were accepted. Eliza was accepted for being one of the eight students in the school's forty year history to have ever aced its entrance exams. Of course, this was partially due to her Furyx vision and a well-placed cheat sheet.

In the middle of the afternoon, thousands of freshmen gathered to say hello to their brand new lives. It was a beehive of activity. Parents were crying. Teenagers that still looked like middle school students ran to and from, marveling at the massive stone Gothic architecture. The school was laid out in a design very similar to England's ancient classic universities. Replicas of famous statues and structures that were destroyed during the last world war lined the many common areas, fields, parking lots and courtyards in front of the building entrances.

Rock bands had gathered to put on mini concerts on the fields, advertising and picking new recruits to their fan bases. Some undergrads were holding martial arts and weapons demonstrations in a forum. The fraternities at the Medici were world-renowned for their brilliant swordsmanship. So holding demonstrations out in the open was perfect for planting the seeds in young freshmen to pledge.

Eliza walked amongst the best and brightest young adults on her way to Cherry Hall for registration. She wasn't surprised to catch the several packs of males staring her way. Everyone wondered how old she was, or if she was even a freshmen. With all its glamour, glitz and exciting atmosphere that made the cold air warm, none of it mattered to Eliza. College was nothing more than what it was supposed to be in her eyes. It was a means to project stability and a normal persona for a young adult.

In Cherry Hall, the lines stretched over the length of a football field that curved around corners and outside the building. Natural soft daylight poured through the high windows near the ceiling. There were four main lines, divided by 6 or more letters of the alphabet. Eliza's line was A through F. She stood mostly amongst the fathers waiting in place of their scions…those scions that filed into their new dorms and drooled over the bands of guys who looked like girls. Like always, Eliza was wearing her light green long hooded overcoat. She controlled an mp3 player in her pocket, slightly bobbing her blonde head to Korean hip hop music from her ear buds. A folder full of printed documents was nicely tucked in her armpit.

At about sixteen registrars till her turn, five busty blond sorority girls stole Eliza's attention. They were all skipping down the hall, loud and obnoxiously overly excited, hugging each other with congratulations to share. Eliza watched as they came down the hall and continued past her toward an exit. Instinctively, she rolled her eyes, wondering if she'd have to put up with that sort of element for the next four years.

"Ridiculous right?"

Through her ear buds, Eliza heard a voice that seeped through. "It's like all they signed up for is to join Capp Silla Con, right?" Eliza found the voice's cynicism amusing and was compelled to turn around and put a face to it.

He was a boyishly handsome young man with stone-gray colored eyes, curly light-brown hair and freckles that were beginning to blend in with his white complexion. He was about half an inch shorter than Eliza but flaunted an aura of maturity. The graphic red hoodie he was wearing had some kind of graffiti expression on the front of it. A theme of modern art reminiscent of the Parisian artists of the 21st century. A thick green book bag was hooked under both arms like a true boy scout, but from the way he smirked so blatant and condescending…

He extended his hand to Eliza and greeted, "Hi, I'm Robby. Robby McCloud."

Eliza nodded, approving his introduction. "Eliza." She uttered before turning back around to continue moving with the line.

"Eliza's a pretty name." Robby complemented. "You don't look like you're from out of state. What high school did you go to?"

It was Eliza's first conversation with anyone her age in a while. So taking out her ear buds, she engaged. "Oh. I um… I've actually been out of the country for the past few years. But once upon a time I was a freshman at C. Taylor High in Tampa Heights."

Robby smiled brightly. "Ah! Okay then! Well welcome back. I didn't go to that high school but I heard about it. It was always on the news for its gang fights and street races."

"Yeah, it was pretty scary for like, the six weeks that I went there." Eliza told him.

"Well, I'm sure you'll find that a lots changed since then." Robby told her.

"Really?" Eliza inquired with a slight skepticism.

"No. No, not really." Robby said, shaking his head no. Eliza chuckled, genuinely surprised by his dry wit.

"I tell you what though, why don't I take you out tonight and fill you in on what you've missed out on?" Robby said, extending his invitation.

Eliza was finally at the desk for registration. And it was perfect timing. That's not to say Eliza felt awkward about the proposal, but she just didn't see it coming. The administrator asked for her name. "Elizabeth Christie." She answered.

Upon hearing the name, Robby furrowed his eyebrows. It was that unnerving feeling that he couldn't put his finger on. He had heard the name before but couldn't place the where or when. It was weird. He wondered why the name bothered him so much, but it did. He was mentally racking his brains so furiously, that he didn't even hear Eliza calling his name.

"Robby?" Eliza called out.

"Yes!" Robby barked with surprise.

Eliza smirked. "I'm sorry. But with this being my first week back, I'd rather just take it easy ya know? But I sincerely appreciate the thought. So thank you." Then she turned back around to check on the progress of her paperwork.

Robby scoffed with a smile before shaking his head, failing to hide the feeling that his mind was just blown. "Wow. That has got to be the nicest rejection…ever. Was not expecting that."

Eliza nods, agreeing with him and proud of herself. "Well, you should still get credit for trying." She smirked.

The administrator gave Eliza a small micro disc containing her class schedule and book suggestions and told her that she was set. After turning around to give Robby final a nod Eliza headed on her way down the hallway. Robby watched her, overwhelmed by her stunning green eyes and slightly mysterious demeanor. Again, his mind raced to find so many answers to the questions that surrounded her. Thus, he was unaware that a frustrated administrator was calling his name.

Out on a wide stone-paved courtyard, students had gathered with their parents to go over brochures of features from the school. Eliza sat on the wide smooth marble ledge of a massive water fountain that acted as a centerpiece for the courtyard. On her computer tablet, she shifted through the numerous brochures of building titles, payment schedules and graduation dates. It excited her to think that it was only the beginning. She briefly pondered if she should enter a sorority, then dismissed the thought after remembering the blonde models from earlier.

"Alright, so I know what you're thinking…"

Amongst the ambiance of laughter and various conversations of families, a clear voice called out to her once again. Eliza looked up to see Robby hovering above her. His presence was beginning to annoy her.

"Didn't I get rid of you already?" She thought to herself.

"I'm not stalking you." Robby said with the same smirk from earlier.

Eliza forced a polite smile on as Robby sat beside her and pulled out a laptop. Eliza continued reading over her brochures but occasionally glanced over to see what Robby was doing. She noticed that he was registering with the school on his laptop.

"If you could register online, then why did you wait in that line?" Eliza had to know.

"They still need your written signature. I wanted to go ahead and get that out of the way." Robby said as he examined a file on his laptop.

"Where are your parents?" Eliza asked.

Robby didn't answer, but continued typing. Eliza began to wonder if Robby had picked up on her apathy. She didn't dislike him. She just wanted to be alone. She was used to being alone. She did however appreciate his friendly demeanor and the fact that he felt comfortable in speaking with her. Just as she decided to open up, Robby asked a question that was so far from left field. A question so completely unexpected. It immediately put Eliza on edge.

"You're Emil Christie's daughter. Aren't you?" Robby asked.

"What…" Eliza's stare gradually turned to a squinty green-eyed glare of spite.

"My old man was a former Imperial Intelligence officer stationed in Miami. I've been hacking into the Imperial databases since I was thirteen. Could've earned the title of a Class A hacker at the Harvard Tech tournament a couple years back. But if you even make it past the first level, then you have to register with the ICPA. Imperial Cyber Police Agency. And I just don't like the government getting a lock on me, ya know?" Robby told her.

"Your dad was an intelligence officer?" Eliza asked.

Robby nodded, still typing nonstop. "He was done in last year by the syndicate. My mom went insane and had to quit her job due to fits of hysteria. Officially, she's been diagnosed with dementia. She's with a nursing home back in Dade County."

Robby stopped typing and turned to Eliza with a serious expression. "I heard about you years ago. My dad admired your dad. I know what you're going through. Or, sorry, what you went through." Robby told her.

Eliza sighed deeply. "I doubt that, Robby. But I'm sorry for your loss."

"Braden Pierce?" Robby asked. The name instantly sent electricity through Eliza's veins, standing the hairs on her arms.

"What?" Eliza calmly asked.

"The dependency on law enforcement to uphold the laws in Florida and certain parts of the empire has diminished. The police can't even protect themselves, let alone civilians. Whether it is with swords or bullets, the criminal element has them completely outmanned, outnumbered and overwhelmed in terms of power and strength. Braden Pierce himself is a lone pillar that stands atop the fascist ideals politicians had in mind when they made the United States into the American Empire." Robby explained.

Robby turned his laptop to face Eliza. It showed a profile on Braden Pierce with a question mark in place of where his photo or mug shot should be. "I read your description of your father's murderer and it's definitely Braden. A Detective Inspector named Angel Gazi is in charge of investigating the Pierce Corporation's alleged involvement with the syndicate. But Det. Gazi has his hands full. This profile is a list of activities from witnesses who describe a character that remotely resembles Braden. All of those witnesses are dead now. There isn't any proof that Braden is even related to Isaac Pierce. Everything is purely circumstantial." Robby told her.

"Is Braden the one who killed your father?" Eliza asked.

Robby turned his computer back to himself as he shook his head no. "Nah, my father didn't get that honor. He was poisoned. Even with the few investigative skills I got, I still haven't figured out anything conclusively. I suspect it was a woman though. The day before he died he said that he was supposed to be meeting a new assistant. A woman who kind of matches the description of an infamous Black Creek assassin. Black Creek of course also being under the wings of Pierce Corp. But that's all I got." Robby told her.

Eliza took in his revelation. It was all so astounding. With the different options in front of her, she decided it was best to stick to her own problems. She quickly closed the brochures on her electronic tablet and signed off. As she stood ready to walk off, she told him, "I'm sorry to hear about your loss, Robby. You seem like a decent human being. You deserve better."

Robby looked up to her with a sly grin. He couldn't put his finger on it, but deep down he knew Eliza was about more than she was willing to reveal. With the idea sparked, Robby couldn't help but plant the seed and see how far Eliza was willing to go with it. He went back to typing as he spoke.

"Yeah. I'm sure you and me. We're a dime a dozen. All I can do is monitor Braden's movements through the camera feeds of his known hang outs and keep sending anonymous tips to Gazi."

Eliza stopped in mid-stride and stood pondering. Slowly, she turned back to look at Robby. Her lightly glossed lips slowly curled into a gentle smile. Very politely, she asked, "Do you know where he'll be tonight?"

About the Author –

Revenge, Rivalry and Rebellion, Stage in the Sky is the theater that presents the entertaining stories and essays of neo-romanticist Rock Kitaro.

When I was fifteen, I read three books that would forever change my life. The most significant was Nancy Springer's "I am Mordred." If you know your Arthurian Legend then you know that Mordred is the name of the knight who kills King Arthur. But Nancy Springer's book told the story from Mordred's point of view. It told of his upbringing, his love, his ambitions.

It was amazing. Reading her book opened my eyes to the world of perspective. Before this, and even now, it seems so many people these days forget that there are two sides or more sides to every story. Even the worst villains are heroes to somebody else. No one just rolls out of bed with a desire to cause harm. And even if they do, there's a reason. So why not let the audience decide if that reason is good enough. This is what I do with my stories.

I'll go ahead and tell you that with my stories, I curse and can sometimes be choreographic with my fight scenes. Inspired by Lord Byron, all of my main characters are troubled individuals. They are sophisticated, arrogant, seductive, disrespectful of authority, self-destructive and struggle with a sense of integrity, what's right or wrong.

Make sure to visit www.stageinthesky.com for Rock Kitaro's latest releases or send your regards to RockKitaro@gmail.com.

The Three Kings of Ybor Saga –

Vo1. 1 – Eliza Christie's Vendetta

Vol. 2 – The Wolves of the Syndicate

Vol. 3 – A Reunion of Beasts

Vol. 4 – August the 18th

Vol. 5 – The Kennedy St. Massacre

Vol. 6 – Beware of Romanticists

Vol. 7 – The Ides of March

www.ingramcontent.com/pod-product-compliance
Lightning Source LLC
Chambersburg PA
CBHW070508130626
46555CB00003B/1212